T0303505

# DANCING ON BLADES

"Zalka takes us across the Óperencías sea to a fantastical world rich with magical golden fruits, shape-shifting apples, Glass Mountains, mysterious music, and devils good and bad. Her archival research and translation bring a vibrancy to this collection of engaging tales that otherwise would have remained dormant. The commentary provides interesting perspective to contextualize the stories within Hungarian folkways, making this treasury of interest to both the folklore scholar and the casual lover of really good stories. I will use this book for entertainment, reference, and inspiration."

—Adam Booth,
storyteller and Instructor of Appalachian
folklore and storytelling, Shepherd University

"Like a hand-painted Easter egg, this book delights at every turn."

—Yvonne Healy,
storyteller, past president, National Storytelling Network

# Dancing on Blades

## Rare and Exquisite Folktales From the Carpathian Mountains

Csenge Virág Zalka

Parkhurst Brothers Publishers
MARION, MICHIGAN

**www.parkhurstbrothers.com**

Parkhurst Brothers books are distributed to the trade through the Chicago Distribution Center. Trade orders may be placed through Ingram Book Company, Baker & Taylor, Follett Library Resources and other book industry wholesalers. To order from Chicago Distribution Center, phone 1-800-621-2736 or send a fax to 800-621-8476. Copies of this and other Parkhurst Brothers Publishers titles are available to organizations and corporations for purchase in quantity by contacting Special Sales Department at our home office location, listed on our web site. Manuscript submission guidelines for this publishing company are available at our web site.

Printed in the United States of America

First Edition, 2018

2018 2019 2020 2021 2022 2023 12 11 10 9 8 7 6 5 4 3 2 1

Library of Congress Cataloging in Publication Data is on file and available upon request

ISBN: Hardback 978162491-103-3
ISBN: e-book 978162491-104-0

Parkhurst Brothers Publishers believes that the free and open exchange of ideas is essential for the maintenance of societal freedoms. We support the First Amendment of the United States Constitution and encourage all citizens to study all sides of public policy questions, making up their own minds.

Page design by: Susan Harring Design
Cover design by: Linda D. Parkhurst
Original cover illustration by: Jámbor Katalin
Proofread by Bill and Barbara Paddack
Acquired for Parkhurst Brothers Inc., Publishers
and edited by: Ted Parkhurst

022018

# Acknowledgments

I extend a heartfelt thank you to Magyar Zoltán and Benedek Katalin from the Hungarian Academy of Sciences, who helped me achieve the seemingly impossible – tracking down the manuscripts of Szirmai Fóris Mária. I also thank the staff of the Archives of the Museum of Ethnography in Budapest for helping me locate and copy Pályuk Anna's tales. They were courteous and patient with a stumbling first-time researcher.

I owe gratitude to my oldest friend, Jámbor Katalin, for creating the beautiful cover art for this book, following my detailed requests every step of the way, and helping this volume reflect the visual richness of Pályuk Anna's tales.

I would like to thank my amazing storytelling friends – Adam Booth, Jeri Burns, Janice Del Negro, Diane Edgecomb, Cathryn Fairlee, Lyn Ford, Mary Hamilton, Yvonne Healey, Megan Hicks, and Joseph Sobol – for their endorsements of the manuscript. I am especially grateful to Adam Booth and Mary Hamilton for their detailed comments; they went above and beyond in their reading and helped me weed out numerous typos, grammatical mistakes, and inconsistencies. I am also grateful to Barbara Schutzgruber for talking me through some spinning-related translation issues.

My mother, Bartek Bernadette, shared her love and talent for gardening with me so I could bring the flowers in these tales to life. These stories would not be the same without her.

I owe a debt to storytellers and audiences who appreciated these tales when I told them. Their reactions and suggestions helped me polish them and inspired me to share them in English so that they can travel. And, most importantly, I am eternally grateful to Ted Parkhurst for placing trust in my pet project and helping this book to be born.

## Table of Contents

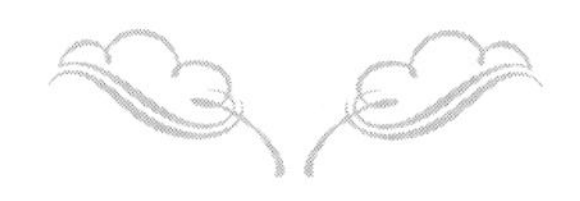

# "Anica, Tell Us a Story!"

*Pályuk Anna and the world of Transcarpathian folktales*

I was a beginner storyteller, bright eyed and bushy tailed, when I came across a plain-looking library book titled *Felsőtiszai népmesék* (*Folktales from the Upper Tisza region*). I was looking for new stories to tell. I sought colorful, delicious, little known Hungarian folktales that had not yet been overdone and contained more than dashing princes chopping off exponentially multiplying dragon heads. I found them in that book. In fact, I found several of them and, looking beyond the individual tales, I became curious. Who told these stories? Why were they so unique, so unlike other folktales I had read? Skipping to the Afterword, written by folklorist Kovács Ágnes[1], I found that the book contained (mixed together) tales from two storytellers, one male, and one female, who lived in the same village more than a hundred years ago. Poring over the Table of Contents, my suspicions were confirmed. All the tales that put stars in my eyes came from only one of the storytellers, and her name was Pályuk Anna.[2]

All I knew about Pályuk Anna came from the Afterword in that one book. She was born in Alsóveresmart (Mala Kopanya, Ukraine) around the middle of the 19th century, possibly in 1858, from a Rusyn family. Rusyns (or Ruthenes), an Eastern Slavic group, formed the ethnic majority of the village over Hungarians, Germans, and some Jewish families. Kovács states that Anna must have been a gorgeous woman in her youth because her first marriage was the stuff of fairy tales. One day, an important man visited her village. His chariot driver, after taking one look at her, sent people with a marriage proposal as soon as he returned home. They had a whirlwind wedding one week later. Anna moved from Veresmart to Tiszabökény (Tiszobikeny, Ukraine), a predominantly Hungarian village, some twenty miles downriver. She lived there for the rest of her life. Even though her young husband died soon after, she stayed on as a maid, first caring for children and later working as a cook. She was over forty years old when she married again. This time, she was married to the richest landowner in the village. Anna spent the rest of her days cheerfully smoking her beloved pipe, telling enchanting tales to a brood of stepchildren and grandchildren who sat at her feet. The collector notes that she never quite lost her Rusyn accent, but when she was telling her stories, all the pronunciation mistakes disappeared, and she spoke the most eloquent Hungarian. She died at the age of 93.

By now, you might be able to see why I had a bit of a problem with the title of this book. I originally called it "Rare and Exquisite Hungarian Folktales," and yet, Anica (as the children called Anna) was more than "just" Hungarian and so were her stories. Furthermore, "Folktales from Hungary" also sounded overly simplistic once I took the history of her home region into consideration.

There is a trick history question that has been featured in our high school graduation exams: *"An old woman has lived in three countries in her lifetime, and yet she never left her house. Where does the house stand?"* That old woman could have been Anna at the time when her stories were collected. Ugocsa County, historically a part of the Hungarian Kingdom for centuries, was split between Czechoslovakia and Romania after the end of World War I. The First and Second Vienna Awards returned Transcarpathia (and Ugocsa in it) to Hungary for the duration of World War II. However, since we were on the losing side of the conflict again, the county was restored to its pre-1938 boundaries after the war's end. Soon after, the Czechoslovakian part was handed over to the Ukraine where it belongs today, including both Pályuk Anna's birthplace and her home village. Therefore, technically, after moving from her Rusyn village to a Hungarian one, Anna lived in three different countries between the ages of 60 and 93 without ever leaving her house.

This was the same period (1915-1950) when Szirmai Fóris Mária, first as a high school student and then as a mature and dedicated collector, gathered and recorded all of Anna's tales. Szirmai was also born in Tiszabökény and listened to the stories of the elders as a child, scribbling them down between classes and returning to collect more of them later as an adult. Kovács Ágnes, a folklorist who edited the first book containing these stories and judged Szirmai's collecting techniques, noted that she should be considered a traditional informant herself. She wrote down many of Anna's tales from memory, editing very little, but no doubt re-wording some parts and patching up others. This first book, the one I found in the library, only contained 30 of Anna's tales, but it hinted that more than a hundred had been collected and archived.

I told Pályuk Anna's tales many times, and they worked like a charm with all audiences. Eventually, they became a signature part of my repertoire as a storyteller, and I found a lot of joy in telling them. For years, the knowledge that there were more where these came from kept nagging at the back of my mind like rumors of treasure hidden in the woods. Finally, I went on my own adventure to find them. I received a research permit for the Archives of the Hungarian Museum of Ethnography, purchased a photo ticket, and—after accidentally locking myself out of the research room twice—I managed to dig up the rest of the collection. It was a true treasure trove of amazing fairy tales, meticulously typed, hand-edited, and submitted to the National Folklore Collection Contest. Most of them were never published. I not only learned more from them about the world of Transcarpathian folktales, but also discovered a lot about the storyteller herself.

Pályuk Anna learned her stories from various people. Her mother and grandmother are mentioned many times. I left some of these comments in the stories, so you can read them for yourself. Occasionally she also credits her father, who went to war when she was little and returned from faraway places with new stories to tell. Traditionally, military service was one of the contexts where storytelling happened, usually in the evenings after curfew. Sharing accommodations with strangers and being stationed far away from home, men exchanged tales, heard new ones, and took them back to their own villages–if they were lucky enough to return. Many of these tales took root in their new homes and flourished in the oral tradition.

Transcarpathia provides an amazingly rich cultural soil for unique stories. Multiple ethnicities and cultures–Hungarian, Rusyn, Romanian, Roma, Jewish, Slovak, German, etc.–have existed together there for centuries. Pályuk Anna's own personal story is proof that the tales often crossed cultural and linguistic boundaries and mingled together, creating a magical world modeled after the Transcarpathian landscape, both in the cultural and the natural sense. Traces of the flora, fauna, and imagery of the Carpathians can be found in many of Anna's tales. Alsóveresmart, her home village, lies at the foot of the famous Black Mountain, now part of the UNESCO East Carpathian Biosphere Reserve. It is covered in old oak forests and bedecked with rare species of wildflowers. The southern slopes of the mountain sport rich vineyards and, on one of its cliffs, stand the ruins of a castle built in the 13th century. Plows and shovels have been known to turn Roman era golden jewelry and old swords out of the soil. As a child, Anna inhabited the same world her tales portray with ancient castles hidden in deep forests, nameless flowers growing over buried treasure, and folk beliefs of dragons, witches, and fairies still very much alive long into the 20th century. Moving downriver, she left the mountains behind for the plains, but she never forgot them. It was in honor of this enchanting landscape that I subtitled this book "Folktales from the Carpathian Mountains," signifying all the cultural and natural diversity represented in these stories and alluding to the name of the region – Transcarpathia (literally, "beyond the Carpathian Mountains").

"Rare and exquisite" also felt appropriate. Many of Pályuk Anna's folktales are unique. Many do not belong to any internationally recognized type.[3] She seems to have been a true artist of the oral tradition, taking symbols, motifs, and elements from fairy tales and re-assembling them into new stories. It is impossible to tell how many of those she inherited from her parents and grandparents, and how many were truly her own creation - but that is the beauty of a living oral tradition.

Some of the texts I found in the Archives seemed jumbled; bits and pieces were out of order and important elements were lost halfway through the plot. Some of the confusions appeared to stem from the storyteller herself. She was growing old at the time of collection. There were parts framed with "oh, I forgot to tell you," or "I probably didn't mention that…" Others might have been the result of Szirmai Fóris Mária's methods, since she wrote down many of the tales from her early memories, fixing them up a little where they had loose parts. Whatever the case, some tales ended up in the Archives somewhat tattered. However, once I began telling them on the stage, they soon righted themselves and came alive with parts clicking into place or emerging to fill in the torn story fabric. This is the reason why I decided not to translate them word for word from the Archives for this book. Rather, I aimed to restore them to their spoken glory, taking some artistic license as the next link in the chain of tradition that has passed them down.

This book does not aim to be an academic publication. I am not a trained folklorist nor do I pretend to be one. I merely use some of their methods to track down tales that intrigue me and find out more about from where the tales came. I am, first and foremost, a performing storyteller. Therefore, the texts in this book are my re-tellings of Pályuk Anna's tales. They are close to her text and delivery, but restored to what they once might have been and written with contemporary, live audiences in mind. In the Comments after each story, I aim to point out the bigger structural changes I have made, or the parts that I kept intact because they amazed or amused me. I also included explanations for certain translation choices. I believe this is enough to make the book an entertaining read and a good resource for storytellers of all kinds. If you are conducting more in-depth folkloristic research and need to delve deeper into details, feel free to find me online. I am happy to help.

These tales have been handed down and preserved for us by a succession of exceptional women. Sadly, all of them–Kovács Ágnes, Szirmai Fóris Mária, Pályuk Anna–are gone now. So are the nameless mothers and grandmothers that passed these tales on to Anna, and her father who managed to salvage the humanity of storytelling from the horrors of war. I dedicate this volume to their memory in the hopes that new storytellers, both women and men, will pick up these tales, find beauty in them, and carry them on.[4]

**Notes**

1. I use all names in this book in their original Hungarian order: Family name(s) first.
2. In case you were wondering, the other storyteller included in the book was a man named Furicz János, about the same age as Pályuk Anna, who lived in Tiszabökény all his life and was regarded as a very popular entertainer. His tales, while they didn't grab my attention as much as Anna's, are also enchanting. I found quite a few of them in the Archives, and some of them are very much worth telling. I hope that, in a future book, I will be honored with the chance to translate them, too. I will mention them here and there in the Comments for comparison to Pályuk's stories.
3. You will notice that many of my Comments refer to folktale types marked with an ATU number. This number refers to the Aarne-Thompson-Uther classification system (see *Sources and Further Reading* at the end of this book). Knowing a folktale's type number can help you locate tales with a similar plot and basic structure from multiple other cultures.

4. In case you are a storyteller entangled in the ethics of our trade, this is an explicit permission for you to tell these tales on the stage, to your children, your students, or to anyone else who you think would enjoy them. However, my publisher reminds me to share the caveat that these stories, as a body of work or individually, may not be recorded or printed in any form (except for brief passages quoted in academic papers), without prior written permission from Parkhurst Brothers Publishers, whose permissions department may be contacted at the address found online at www.parkhurstbrothers.com.

# Part One

## Spinning Old into Gold

The majority of Pályuk Anna's tales don't fall into any recognized folktale type. She builds her own repertoire from symbols and motifs more often than re-telling entire plots. But even when she does work with old stories, her personality, empathy, and love for embellishment shine through. This first chapter contains examples of Anna re-telling well-known fairy tales, her unique voice ringing loud and clear even at the distance of a long and eventful century.

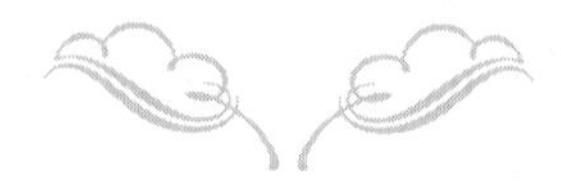

# The Shoe-Shredding Princesses

Once upon a time, far, far across the Óperenciás Sea, there was a great kingdom with a very good king–a king who was always in a somber mood. If someone asked him what ailed him, his eyes filled up with tears. Even though he never told anyone the reason, they could guess easily enough. The King had no son, you see. He did have seven beautiful daughters, but they grew up neglected and did whatever they wished. Their father paid no attention to them in his desperate longing for a male heir. With their wild behavior, they brought much shame and disapproval on his old, grey head, but he resolved to bear it… he could not exile his own beloved daughters, after all.

It was a visit from the royal shoemaker that finally shook the King up from his self-pity. One day, the old craftsman planted himself in front of the throne and took a deep, heroic breath.

"Your Highness, be it my life or my death, I cannot keep silent any longer! The treasurer refuses to buy more leather, the shopkeeper has no more credit for wooden pegs, and I am on the verge of starving to death along with my entire family. I am truly sorry Your Majesty. I cannot keep up with making new shoes for the Princesses to replace the ones they use up every day."

The King was taken aback by this report. How could his daughters use up a new pair of shoes in a day? His own boots lasted a lot longer than that. Granted, he rode a horse sometimes instead of walking...

but still. How could they possibly ruin them so fast? The only plausible explanation was that the shoemaker was lying. The King decided to test him. The next morning, he visited the workshop to look at the brand-new slippers before they were delivered to the Princesses. All seven pairs were so beautiful, so masterfully made, that the old King laughed as he inspected them.

"These shall last them a month, at least, even if they wear them all day. Even if they sleep in them!"

"No, they will not, Your Majesty," the shoemaker shook his head mournfully. "By tomorrow morning their soles and heels will be gone, and even the leather will be torn."

*That's impossible!* thought the King. And to keep the shoemaker from replacing them in secret, he put a mark inside all the shoes in a place where the Princesses could not see it. But come the next morning, the King was terribly shocked. Everything was as the shoemaker had said. All the shoes had been shredded to pieces. That is, all except for one pair. The youngest Princess's shoes were in pristine condition.

The King was baffled by the mystery. He tried to solve it by other methods at first. He spent his entire day with his daughters, for the first time in his life, watching their feet like a hawk. Come evening, the slippers were not even dusty, let alone torn. But even though the Princesses were locked into their room all night under seven locks, watched by seven guards, and with their governess listening for suspicious sounds, they still left somehow and returned by morning with their shoes destroyed. Where did they go? What did they do? It was impossible to tell. Since he could find no explanation, the King announced to his subjects that whoever could discover where and how the Princesses were shredding their shoes would be rewarded with half his kingdom and even one of the Princesses for a wife, if he so wished. Royalty was a lot cheaper back in the day, you see. To balance the scales, the King also announced that whoever tried *and failed* to solve the puzzle would pay with his life.

Despite the looming threat of execution, the court filled with willing knights, wise men, and all kinds of crafty travelers. But no one could uncover the Princesses' secret. One hundred young men lost their heads in the affair, and the people of the kingdom started to grumble and complain about so many deaths. Even the King himself felt sorry for all the promising young lives lost, but he could not go back on his word. He announced that he did not care where the volunteers came from or what tricks and crafts they used. He wanted to know where his daughters were shredding their shoes and that was *all* he cared about.

Once again, the court filled with all kinds of wanderers. But none of them could bring back any results, and more innocent lives were lost. The Princesses were smart and cautious. They mixed sleeping powder into the food of anyone who wished to spy on them at night. Each morning, shredded shoes piled up outside the castle gates for everyone to see; it was all the kingdom talked about now. People discussed the mystery everywhere, from the royal kitchens to the farthest mountain pastures.

One day, a young shepherd came to the castle and said to the King, "Your Majesty, my life is in your hands and so is my death. I volunteer to guard the Princesses tonight. I only ask two things. First, if I fail tonight, allow me to try two more times. In exchange, I promise that if I succeed by the third try, I will not ask for your kingdom nor one of your daughters. The second thing I ask is that you allow me to take my spotted piglet into the Princesses' bedroom with me."

"What a foolish request from a foolish boy," the King muttered. "Sure, let it be as you wish. We have never had a piglet sleep in the royal bedrooms anyway."

The young shepherd hid the piglet under his fur cloak, and as he sat at the dinner table with the Princesses, he fed everything from his plate to the animal. He never ate a bite. As dinner was nearing its end, he suddenly felt the piglet kick, then go limp.

*This would have been me if I had eaten anything*, the shepherd thought angrily. He remembered the three pieces of advice his mother had left him when she died (because she had nothing else to leave): "*Never eat from the table of noblemen; never look back; always share what you have with someone poorer than yourself.*" This was why he didn't eat a bite, because princesses, although women, were nobility, too. And now his piglet was dead. He mourned it more than any person. He held it gently in his arms as he pretended to sleep.

Around midnight, he heard the Princesses getting out of bed. They told their younger sister to check on the shepherd to see if he was asleep. The youngest Princess returned to them saying that he was sleeping so deeply, he had even smothered that piglet he was cuddling. There was pity in her voice. The shepherd swallowed his bitterness, and lay quietly as the Princesses got dressed.

When they were all ready to go, the seven girls pushed the wardrobe out of the way, revealing a trap door behind it. Agreeing to leave it open–no one was going to notice it anyway–they all filed through the door and down a flight of stairs. As soon as they were gone, the shepherd lay the piglet in the youngest Princess's bed, tucked it in, and followed them underground.

When they reached the bottom of the stairs, the girls broke into a wild run. They ran and they ran far, far away until they reached a forest entirely made of copper. The shepherd reached up and broke off a leaf. The trees rang out and chimed, but all the Princesses–except for the youngest–waved it off.

"It is only the wind. Come on!"

The youngest Princess glanced behind her back, but she said nothing. She was the kindest and the smartest of them all.

They ran on and on until they reached a forest made of silver. The shepherd broke off a leaf here, too, and this time the Princesses stopped and searched for the intruder for a while. But the shepherd had a fur cloak that, when he turned it inside out, made him impossible to notice. Finally, the sisters gave up the search and ran on until they arrived at a forest made of gold. The shepherd broke off a leaf again, but this time the Princesses didn't even stop. They were too eager to make it to the splendid castle that stood in the middle of the forest. The gates slammed shut behind them, and the shepherd could not follow them inside.

He sunk the leaves into his pocket and walked around the castle. Finding a large window, he peered in. He could see the Princesses sitting about a round table, feasting, and listening to music so beautiful that even the angels in heaven could not have sung better. Soon a door opened and in walked seven handsome knights, each taking a seat next to one of the Princesses. The Princesses and the young knights ate together, talked together, and laughed together. When they were done feasting, at the signal of the eldest Knight, they all stood up to dance–all except for the youngest Princess, who refused to join in. The dance was so wild it made the walls of the castle tremble. As the shepherd looked closer, he found the answer to the mystery of the shredded shoes. The floor of the ballroom was made of gleaming scythe blades, straightened and stacked closely together. The slippers fell to pieces right in front of his eyes. It was a miracle that the feet of the Princesses were not shredded, too.

It was almost dawn when the dance ended. The Princesses prepared to leave. The Knights begged them with tears in their eyes to visit twice more, and all would be well. The Princesses promised; the shepherd realized he would have to follow them for two more nights to find out what would happen in the end. He had to run at full speed to make it to his own bed before the Princesses arrived home, slamming the wardrobe back to its place.

As the youngest Princess got into her bed, she let out a startled scream.

"What happened?" her sisters asked in the dark, but she waved them off.

"Nothing, I just hit my foot on this feather pillow."

She picked up the pillow, together with the pig, and put it down on top of the shepherd who was lying on the floor by her bed.

As she did so, she leaned down to whisper, "Don't put a pig in my bed again!"

The next morning, when the King woke up, the shepherd was already standing under his window.

*He must know something!* the King thought. But when he asked, the shepherd told him he'd found out nothing at all; he would have to sleep in the Princesses' bedroom again. The King agreed, warning the shepherd that he only had two nights left.

That evening at dinner, the Princesses piled food on the shepherd's plate, one delicious dish after another. This time, he had his puli dog hiding under the fur cloak. None of the girls suspected him, except for the youngest, who already sensed that the shepherd knew more than he let on. As she served his food, she slipped a tiny key into his palm.

After dinner had dragged on and on, the shepherd felt his puli dog go limp in his lap. *These are not decent people*, he thought bitterly to himself as he lay down. *I would not marry any of them, even if they had gold stars shining on their foreheads. I'd rather marry Julis, from the neighbor's house, than any of these Princesses with a mountain of gold for a dowry.*

As soon as dinner was over, the Princesses ran to the trap door under the wardrobe. When they wanted to close the door behind them, they realized the key was missing. They pulled the door closed from the outside, but the shepherd opened it again with the key as soon as they were gone and followed them like the night before. Everything happened the same way, except for the youngest Princess, who was scolded repeatedly by her sisters for losing the key and possibly locking them out of their home. The shepherd only had time to slip through and jump into bed before they all returned. As the youngest Princess got into her bed, she screamed again.

"What is it this time?" grumbled her sisters. "You always make a fuss about something. Go to sleep!"

"I'm sorry," she whispered. Not wanting to admit to her sisters that her bed contained a dead dog, she said, "The washerwoman must have left a pin in my blanket."

With that, she put the dog and the blanket down on top of the shepherd and warned him not to prank her again, or she would tell her sisters, and they would kill him for sure.

The next morning, before the Princesses woke up, the shepherd buried the dog under the King's window and waited for him to look outside. But when the King inquired about what he found out, the shepherd only shrugged and asked for one last night. The King agreed although he was sure that, one way or another, the shepherd would be dead by the morrow.

Things happened the same way on the third night. This time, the shepherd took to dinner with him his raven, a tame bird that ate from his hands, and fed it with all the choice pieces the Princesses piled on his plate. The bird dropped down onto his lap like the pig and the dog before it, and the shepherd pretended to go to sleep, but when he followed the Princesses through the door, he carried the raven with him instead of leaving it in the bed.

It was lucky that he did. As he peered into the ballroom through the window, watching the Princesses dance on blades once again, the bird suddenly stirred. It woke up, broke the glass with its beak, and swooped into the hall - just in the right moment. See, the youngest Princess was still refusing to dance with the youngest Knight, but he would not stop pursuing her. When his sweet words all failed, he tried to drag her to the dance floor by force. The raven descended on him with beak and claws and chased him around the ballroom until it managed to sink its razor-sharp talons into the Knight's eyes. The Knight, blinded, staggered over to a vat of water in the corner, stumbled into it face first, and drowned. Only the youngest Princess and the shepherd saw all this. The others were so absorbed in their dancing that they never noticed a thing.

It was almost dawn when the Princesses returned home. The youngest still had her shoes fresh and untouched. She carefully patted her bed, but there was nothing in it. She couldn't even find the shepherd, who was already hiding under her bed. As the Princesses fell into an exhausted sleep, the shepherd grabbed her untorn shoes and went straight to the King to tell him everything from beginning to end.

"If you are speaking the truth," said the old King, "you will receive every reward I promised. If the Princesses admit that they have been where you say they have, I will give you one of them as a wife, and my kingdom to rule."

The King gathered his entire court and summoned his daughters. He asked them where they had gone to dance every night. The six oldest Princesses denied that they had gone anywhere, and swore on everything holy that they had been in their beds, sleeping, from sundown until morning. The youngest did not say a word.

"What about the door under the wardrobe?" the King demanded. They denied that, too, but their father himself went to their room and had the furniture moved, revealing the trap door. The six older Princesses could not deny its existence anymore. Instead, they claimed that they sometimes snuck out to take a little walk in the gardens, but never went farther.

"And what about the copper forest?" the King asked them. They all stated at once that they have never heard of such a thing. But when the shepherd pulled out the copper leaf, they could deny it no more. They tried to insist that the leaf must have come from some old copper trees growing in some remote corner of the royal gardens. The King carried on, pulling out the silver leaf, then the golden one, and then the untorn shoes of the youngest Princess.

"How come your shoes are not shredded, my darling?" he asked her kindly.

The shocked faces of all seven sisters spoke volumes. The truth came to light at last. The Princesses confessed that they had been cursed by a witch who had tried to marry the King after the death of their mother. When she was rejected by the King, she took her anger out on the girls. They were bound by a spell to run to the castle of the Spirit King every night and dance on blades until dawn. But there were also seven handsome knights there, cursed just like they had been, and the sisters admitted that if their father would let them, they would go back and marry the knights for love.

"Is this what you all want?" demanded the King.

Six of the Princesses answered "YES" as one; but the youngest only bowed her head, tears dripping onto her shoes. Her father patted her cheek gently.

"Do you not want to go back to the Spirit Kingdom, my darling?"

She looked up sadly and answered, "There is no one for me there. And even if there were a prince waiting for me, I wouldn't go, because there is someone here who stole my shoes… and also stole my heart. If he has not left yet, if he has decided to stay, I would remain by his side until the end of my days."

"Well, if you love that brave boy that went to so much trouble because of you, I am happy to give my blessing on your marriage. We'll have a wedding once your sisters have left."

The youngest Princess hugged her father, and he hugged her back. The six older sisters said their goodbyes, walked through the trap door, and disappeared from the castle forever. The trap door was bricked in. There was no more connection to the relatives in the Spirit Kingdom. Everyone agreed that it was better this way.

The shepherd became King, and the youngest Princess became Queen. They had a great wedding that went on for seven days and signaled the beginning of better, happier times. The old shoemaker, who only had to make slippers for the Queen now, and only had to replace them every once in a while, was especially happy.

Once things had settled down, the Queen asked her husband how he managed to discover their secrets, and he told her about the advice he inherited from his mother. Now he could eat from the nobility's table because he was a nobleman himself. The Queen told him he lived through the copper, silver, and golden forests because he never turned around to fight the copper, silver, and gold Knights lurking right behind him, eager for a fight. There was only one piece of advice left to follow: to share half his kingdom with someone poorer than him. Since the Queen did not inherit anything, he decided to share it with her. They lived long and happily, and ruled together side by side.

You know, I only wish they would have given me one of those leaves the shepherd stole. I would have been satisfied with just the copper one. But no, the young King hung all three on the wall to remind everyone of the adventures that led him to the throne. Since neither the King nor the Queen thought of giving them to me instead, my story about them comes to an end right here.

**Comments**

This story was published in two of the collections featuring some of Pályuk Anna's tales, but I could not find the original manuscript in the Archives. While researching it, I read dozens of Hungarian versions of the same type. The tale of the "Dancing Princesses" (ATU 306) is very popular in the Hungarian tradition, especially in the Eastern part of the country.

It usually takes a *much* darker turn. In several texts, the Princesses sneak out to go to a witches' gathering and, when the truth is revealed, they are either imprisoned or executed in various horrible ways for practicing witchcraft. They dance with devils on scythe blades, razorblades, or mirrors (glass shards?), tearing their shoes apart. "Dancing" is also a thinly veiled metaphor for more intimate activities. In some versions, the older sisters are pregnant or have children hidden in the Other World that they feed at night. Therefore, the "untorn shoes" of the youngest Princess signal her innocence in more ways than one. When told by female storytellers, the story is usually somewhat kinder to the girls (go figure), but not many I found were as forgiving and emotionally complex as Pályuk Anna's version.

My re-telling follows the original text closely, with only a few details that needed sorting. At the beginning, the story states that the *King* had men executed if they failed to solve the mystery; but later, it is hinted that the *Princesses* are poisoning the suitors, even though "sleeping powder" is mentioned in the text. In my version, I chose sleep over death, and assumed that the amount of powder that would make a grown man sleep would probably kill a piglet or a small dog. If you find that other explanations suit you better, the story is definitely up for interpretation. Especially if you feel sorry for the pig and the dog, as I do.

The "fur cloak" in the story refers to a *guba*, a staple piece of clothing for Hungarian shepherds. *Puli* is a kind of Hungarian sheepdog, small and shaggy, resembling a mop. The witch that wanted to marry the King, and cursed his daughters, is labeled a *böjti boszorkány*, which is the name of a straw figure that was traditionally set on fire to signal the end of winter. In older beliefs, they appear as powerful witches (the supernatural kind, not mortal women with powers) associated with sinister gatherings that the Princesses frequent in other versions of this tale. This way, even Pályuk Anna's romantic telling retains some of the darker themes of this folktale type.

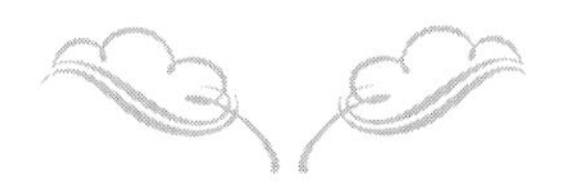

# The Cheerful Prince

Once upon a time, across the Óperenciás Sea, there was a well-ordered little kingdom ruled by a king who was, let's say, far from handsome. And yet, he had a beautiful wife and many beautiful children. In addition to being beautiful, one of his sons was also so cheerful, such a happy child, that he could laugh at anything and everything, and his laughter lit up the whole kingdom. He laughed on the day when his father died, even though he had nothing to be cheerful about. The son was left with the burden of ruling the kingdom, and anyone who thinks kings have no troubles or worries should think again.

One day the Cheerful Prince (who was a king now, but the name had stuck) decided it was time for him to get married. But whom should he wed? It was a big question, not the least because others also had a say in the matter. First and foremost, was his mother, and second, the noblemen of the court. Everyone had an opinion about whom the King should marry, and several of them set out to find the perfect wife for him, in hopes of being richly rewarded for their efforts. One looked for the most beautiful woman in the kingdom; one looked for the kindest; one looked for the wealthiest; and so on. Only the Cheerful Prince did not look for anything. He just walked out of the palace and followed his heart.

It just so happened that he stopped, dizzy from all the walking, in the door of a fisherman's cottage. There he met a girl who was as radiant as the sun and as good as soft butter on warm bread. She could even spin pure gold thread out of the hedge fence! Or so claimed the old woman who was her stepmother. The Cheerful Prince proposed to the girl immediately, despite her father's fretting that she was too young, too poor, and not educated in courtly etiquette. If people laughed at her or made fun of her for not knowing their ways, she might even die of embarrassment. She needed to be loved, the father insisted. She had had a hard-enough life already. But the Cheerful Prince insisted that he would love, cherish, and care for her and that he did not care about whether she knew the rules of etiquette or not. The Cheerful Prince declared that he did not care what anyone thought, except for his own heart.

The Cheerful Prince returned home and told his mother what a beautiful, smart, kind girl he had found. He knew that his mother would be glad for his happiness. But there was another person at court who did not approve of the engagement at all. It was the treasurer, who had hoped that the Cheerful Prince would wed *his* daughter. To sabotage the wedding, the treasurer told the Cheerful Prince and the dowager Queen that a royal bride had to be wealthy, for the good of the kingdom. If the Prince insisted on marrying someone of low birth, then she'd better get to spinning the fence into gold straight away because the treasury was in sore need of funds (which was no wonder, since the treasurer had been filling his own pockets from it for years). Good cheer was not going to keep the coffers full, the treasurer warned them.

With the promise of golden thread unmeasured, the day of the wedding was set.

When the girl found out what her stepmother had said about her to her future husband, she was dismayed. Her father noticed the fear in her eyes and asked her what was wrong. She just leaned on his shoulder and wept so pitifully that his heart almost broke in half. He decided to cheer her up, and went to the river to catch fish for her favorite dishes for a last meal before she was taken away to the palace. As he was casting his net, he suddenly felt a strong tug. When he pulled it in, however, there was only a tiny, gold-colored fish caught in the tangles. The fisherman was surprised that such a tiny fish, barely half a pound, could pull with such force.

As he was about to cast it back, the fish spoke, "Listen to me, good man. Before you put me back, take two scales of mine. Your wife has made a promise that your daughter will never fulfill without my help. On her wedding day, give the scales to her as a gift and tell her to cast one into the fire if she needs help and cast the other if she wants to see you."

The fisherman, speechless, did as he was told. The next day the Cheerful Prince came to fetch his bride. She left behind everything she owned, even her clothes, except for the two tiny fish scales which she tucked into the bodice of her new dress. They went to the palace together, and had a great, cheerful wedding. People rich and poor instantly took a liking to the young Queen, who was not only fair, but also had a kind word for everyone.

Everyone was happy… except for the treasurer. The wedding was barely over when he went to the Cheerful Prince and reported that two piles of fence hedges had been gathered, and he should set the Queen to spinning straight away. The Dowager Queen felt sorry for her daughter-in-law, who was expected to turn switches into golden thread. To hide the young Queen's embarrassment, the dowager Queen ordered it all brought to a private room, so that the girl could work away from prying eyes. *If she can't spin it into gold, we'll figure something out*, the dowager Queen decided.

The fisherman's daughter, now a queen herself, sat all day in the room full of fences, crying her eyes out. She picked pieces up and put them down, but they were useless even for a fence now, let alone for golden thread. In the evening, her cheerful husband came to visit her, and wiped away her tears. He told her to laugh at the folly of the treasurer, but she had no laughter in her heart.

The Cheerful Prince went to his mother and asked her to talk to the treasurer. He insisted that he would not stand for his beloved wife being tortured like this. She was, after all, no demon or witch that would have the power to turn things into gold. The next morning, when the treasurer appeared with two of his men to haul the golden thread away as promised, the clever dowager Queen stood in their path.

"You won't have any thread today," she told them sternly, "I took the first batch for myself. It is only fair that I should have the first of the golden thread made by my daughter-in-law, is it not? Let her rest now, she is tired. Come back tomorrow."

The young Queen was moved to tears by the kindness of her mother-in-law, but also worried what she would say the next day. But the dowager Queen was ready with a new lie the next time the treasurer showed up.

"It is only fair and generous to offer some of the golden thread to the spinsters in our kingdom, don't you think?" asked the Dowager Queen. "I already had it sent over to the House of Unwed Women. You can come back tomorrow."

The treasurer was no fool. He knew that he was being led on, but did not dare argue with the Dowager Queen. Instead, he decided to send others to do his work: the soldiers whose payment was lacking. The treasurer told them to force the King and Queen to immediately give up the golden thread. If they couldn't, he thought, the hungry soldiers would rebel against them, and they would lose the throne and the kingdom.

"Why did your stepmother say you could spin gold, my dear?" the dowager Queen sighed when they were left alone, and the young Queen started weeping again.

The young Queen decided that she should leave her husband, although she loved him, so that he could take a wealthy wife for the good of the kingdom. But as she was getting ready to leave, she felt something shift under her bodice and remembered the fish scales. *Dear God, help me now*, she thought, and tossed one of them into the fire. The next moment, a tiny man stepped out of the flames with a beard so long it trailed after him on the ground.

"What is your wish, Mistress? Whatever it is, it will be done the moment it is said."

"My dear little friend, I am in so much trouble. My stepmother told the Cheerful Prince that I could spin these hedge fences into golden thread. The kingdom is in debt, we need the gold, but I have none, since I am only the daughter of a poor fisherman. The treasurer hates me because he wanted his own daughter to marry the Prince, and now he is torturing my Prince and me for the gold. My mother-in-law is a kind woman, but she can't help us anymore. If you have any advice to give, I'll be eternally grateful to you."

"Well said, my dear. I can give you more than just advice. I'll turn the hedges outside the palace into gold right away and the ones in here as well, so you can tell them you've spun it all. See that old woman over there, with the large floppy hands? Next time you see her, point her out to your husband. Tell him that is what too much spinning will do to your hands. He won't let you do work like that anymore, I promise."

With that, the little man disappeared, and the room was suddenly full of golden thread. It was so brilliant that the young Queen could barely breathe from awe. The people of the court gathered to marvel at the sight. When the treasurer arrived to look, he got hiccups from the surprise. No one had ever heard of such treasures, not even in fairy tales! Even if they started spending the gold right away, it would never run out. When the Cheerful Prince walked in, his face, which had been somber for three days now, lit up with a bright smile. Then he began to laugh, and his laughter made the leaves on the trees dance with joy. It was as if the sun had come out again after long days of dark clouds looming in the sky.

There was nothing to worry about now – there was joy in the kingdom, joy in the young King's eyes, joy in the young Queen's smile, and joy in the heart of the mother-in-law who really loved them both. And just then, an old woman wandered through the door, with large, floppy hands like shovels.

The Cheerful Prince told someone to give the beggar woman food and send her away as he did not want his wife to have to look at someone like that in their hour of celebration. But his surprise was great when the young Queen ran up to the old woman and embraced her.

"Auntie! I am so glad you came!"

The Cheerful Prince stepped closer and asked, "Grandmother… why do your hands look like that?"

"Oh, my dear Cheerful Prince, there is a reason. I have been doing all my life what your young Queen has just done for three days. That is what stretched my hands out like this."

The Cheerful Prince's face lit up, mirroring the mischievous smile in the grandmother's eyes.

He turned to the court and said, "Did you all hear what this old lady just said? Do you want the hands of my beloved wife to look like *that*? Do you want her to keep spinning hedge fences until she is crippled? Answer me! If anyone says yes, they are welcome to leave the kingdom right now, and go far, far away, or else they will have to answer to me!"

The answer was a resounding "NO" from the entire court. They already had enough golden thread to support not one, but two kingdoms. There was no need to torture the young Queen anymore. She was free, and she was finally happy. She took the other golden fish scale and tossed it into the fire. As soon as the tiny man appeared, she asked him to bring her father to court because she missed him dearly. The next moment, there was a knock on the door and the old fisherman joined in the celebration. The Cheerful Prince exiled the treasurer, and put his father-in-law in charge of the gold. He worked hard, and never stole a single coin – unlike his predecessor.

The Cheerful Prince and his wife had three bouncing children, two boys, and a girl. They were all cheerful, just like their father. And they all lived cheerfully ever after.

### Comments

This is quite possibly the most empathic version of "Rumpelstiltskin" (ATU 500) that I have ever come across. It features a cast of lovable characters such as the Cheerful Prince, the clever dowager Queen ("A kind mother-in-law is rare like a white raven," interjects Anna at one point in the story), and the fisherman who proves himself a gentle and caring father. The title character of the classic folktale only plays a secondary role in the drama that unfolds between the ambitious treasurer and the close-knit little family. The emphasis is not on the magic, but on the emotions evoked by an impossible promise and the malice aimed at two young people.

The old woman at the end is a wandering character from a tale that is often attached to Rumpelstiltskin: ATU 501, "The Three Spinners." The Prince's claim that his wife "should not have to look at someone like that" can be read in numerous ways. One way is a comment on the old woman's appearance or a sense of sadness about her condition. Another way is that in Hungarian tradition, pregnant women were not supposed to look at disabled people for the risk of giving birth to a child with a birthmark. So, depending on how one tells the story, the comment can be one of distaste, one of pity, or a hint at the Queen's condition. This is not the only reference to physical appearance in the story either. At the beginning, we learn that the Cheerful Prince's father was "the ugliest man in the world" (which I re-worded as "far from handsome"). Anna balances this out with the claim that he still had a wonderful family and lived a happy life.

The little man, who is usually known as Rumpelstiltskin after the Grimm's version of this fairy tale, is nameless in Pályuk's telling, but has various names in other Hungarian texts. If you wish to give him a name, you can take your pick: Pancimanci, Koppciherci, Tánci Manci, Tánci Vargaluska, Rupcsen-Hercsen, or Turánka (this latter one is a hag). The story is known from more than a dozen sources; those that were collected in Eastern Hungary are almost all mixed with the Three Spinners tale. In most cases, the promise of the first-born child is replaced with the girl offering herself as a bride in exchange for help. This entire dark deal is replaced by kindness in Pályuk's story. I only found one other story from this region where the girl is helped by an older woman without the expectation of a reward. In that tale, from the neighboring Ung County, the grateful young bride told the Prince she had "two mothers" in the end.

I have kept my version close to the original text. I only rearranged a few parts so the logical sequence would make more sense. "Hedge fence" is the term I used for a kind of fence woven from willow switches. "Fish scales" were translated from the Hungarian term *halpénz*, "fish money." While not a term recognized in English, it is interesting to mention since so much of this tale revolves around monetary wealth.

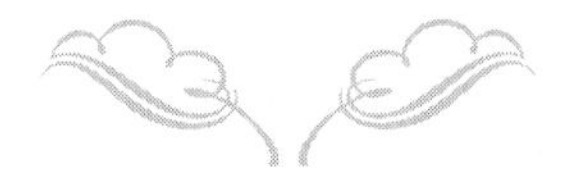

# The Stolen Apples

Once upon a time, a flea's hop beyond the far side of the Óperenciás Sea, there was a great mountain. On top of the mountain lived the White Duke, who had two treasures: his beautiful daughter and a tree of golden apples. Anyone could have thought him happy for those things… and yet he was not happy at all. His daughter was ill, and the only thing that could have cured her was a golden apple from the tree in their own garden. But every time one ripened on the branches, something or some-one stole it overnight.

The mystery brought much suffering to the people. The Duke announced that whoever could guard the fruit of the magic tree would receive half of his wealth and the hand of his daughter in marriage – but whoever failed, would be put on a stake. Despite the terrible warning, all kinds of brave young men volunteered, rich and poor alike, but no one succeeded. One day, a young, ragged soldier came to the castle and saw all the stakes. He asked people what the reason was for so many cruel deaths. He was told about the challenge to guard the magic tree and how the White Duke's anger had killed all who failed.

"I can guard those apples," said the ragged soldier. "Just let me look at the Duke's daughter first, to see if she is worth risking my life."

"You will see her soon enough. They are bringing her right now in a litter," the people pointed. "She is too weak to walk."

And so, it was. The servants carried a litter, and in the litter, lay the sick girl. The soldier walked up, leaned in, and looked at her closely with such familiarity that she let out a startled yelp – the first sound she had made in days.

The soldier spoke to her in a cheerful and soothing voice, "Don't worry one bit, love, we will be eating our fill of golden apples by tomorrow."

People gasped and exchanged shocked glances. Who did this soldier think he was, talking to the Duke's daughter like that? Why was he so sure he could succeed where everyone else had failed?

They did not know that there was a good reason for his confidence. When the soldier set out from home to guard the apple tree, his mother had given him a loaf of fresh bread and the advice that he should share it with any poor soul he encountered on the road. It wasn't long before he sat down at the edge of a forest, eating plain bread (since he had no bacon to go with it), daydreaming about how he'd have bread *and* bacon once he won the Duke's challenge. Suddenly a ragged old man stepped out of the woods right in front of him, teeth chattering and bones rattling from hunger.

"My son, if you give me your bread, I'll help you in whatever venture you are on."

"I will gladly share it with you," the soldier offered. "Let me just take one more slice. I am still hungry."

But the beggar insisted that he'd like the entire loaf.

"Here, have it then, grandfather, eat it all. But I am curious – how can you help me in my endeavor? I am going to the White Duke's castle to volunteer to guard the apple tree."

"That is an easy task, son," the beggar answered between two bites. "Here, take this little handkerchief. When you go to the tree for the night, put it under your head. When you feel the earth move, stand up, and shake this handkerchief twice towards the moon."

*I can do that*, thought the soldier, but the old man was not yet done. He told the soldier to be *sure* to jump up right when the earth moved – otherwise he would fail like all the other guards had failed before him.

That is why the soldier, when he arrived at the castle, was so confident in his chances.

That night, the Duke held a great feast in honor of the latest volunteer. Everyone thought he'd be dead the next day, so they might as well feed him well one last time. But the soldier did not eat a bite—and with good reason. The old beggar had also told him that the cook had been mixing the sleeping powder into the guards' food. He was determined to stay awake for the entire night.

He was escorted with fiddle music to the tree and left there. Tired from the long journey, he was ready to lie down. As he looked up at the sky, with his arms folded behind his head, he could see large black clouds gathering above the tree. He worried for a moment that he would not be able to see the moon, but the moonlight soon broke through, and the clouds dispersed into a flock of black birds. The birds descended onto the tree and began pecking at the apples. The soldier jumped up, waving his arms and yelling at them, until they all fled. Then he sat back down, keeping an eye on the tree in case the birds decided to return. Could it really have been this easy? As time passed, his eyelids began to grow heavy. He was about to fall asleep when he remembered the handkerchief and what the old beggar had told him. He unfolded it and put it under his head, closing his eyes and trusting that an earthquake would wake him.

It was almost midnight when the ground shook with such force that it would have woken the dead, let alone the living. The soldier sprang up, and he saw an enormous giant standing right by the tree, filling his shirt with golden apples. The soldier took the handkerchief and tossed it at the head of the giant, who immediately froze, spellbound, unable to move. The giant started begging for his freedom, offering the soldier one thing after another: the Duke's castle, his lands, his wealth, his daughter, and even an invisible carriage that could fly. The soldier refused to listen. Even though the magic handkerchief held the giant rooted to the spot, he bound the thief with ropes to be sure he wouldn't escape.

When dawn broke, the soldier yelled, "Come and see the apple thief!"

People flocked to the garden to gape at the captured giant and the happily glinting golden apples. As the soldier took the handkerchief off the giant's head, everyone could see that he looked eerily like the royal cook. It soon turned out that the two were related. The cook had disguised himself as a human, and the two giants had been working together to steal the apples and cause death and destruction. The Duke remembered how it had been the cook's suggestion to execute the guards who failed, and the soldier told everyone about the sleeping powder at the feasts.

There was both dismay and laughter in the castle that day. There was dismay from the cook, who was executed together with his wife (even though she was human, and the soldier felt sorry for her). And there was dismay from the giant who was tied to the top of the magic tree so that the birds would peck him apart. The laughter and joy came from the Princess who took only one bite of a golden apple, and she was instantly healed. She wanted to kiss the soldier's hands in gratitude, but he told her he'd rather she kissed his cheeks instead, and she happily complied. They decided to get married straight away since people were already gathered at court to celebrate the capture of the thief.

The soldier brought his mother to court to live with him. He also wanted to find the old beggar, but he was nowhere to be found. So, they held a wedding, had a great feast (made by a new cook, so nobody fell asleep) and lived happily ever after. Golden apples grew by the hundreds from that day on. Maybe they are still growing somewhere. If you want to see them, all you must do is look…

**Comments**

The "Golden apples stolen at night" folktale type is very common in the Hungarian tradition – much more so than in other European countries. It is our very own special flavor for ATU 400, "The Man Who Lost His Bride" (we even gave it its own number, MNK 400A). The way the story usually goes, the King's magical golden apples (or sometimes pears) are stolen every night until one brave man manages to stay awake and capture the thief. The thief usually turns out to be a fairy maiden who falls in love with her captor. When someone meddles with the lovers' idyll, the bride leaves. The hero sets out to find her again and goes through all kinds of adventures until he succeeds in winning her back.

Golden apples are common in Western traditions, whether you think of Idunn's apples from Norse mythology or the garden of the Hesperides from Greek myth. There are also stories from the Caucasian Nart sagas and Carpathian Rusyn traditions that are very much like ours. Hungarian children are generally familiar with the golden apple tale, if not from tradition, then from a famous dramatization by Vörösmarty Mihály (*Csongor és Tünde,* 1830) that is mandatory reading in most grade schools. The folktale type, known as "Prince Árgirus" after the hero's name, according to folklorists is based on a Greek tale that was translated into Hungarian sometime in the 16th century and then entered our oral tradition.

Anna's story is missing the element of the bird-bride; it focuses on the mystery of the stolen apples instead. She creates a whole conspiracy behind the theft, involving the cook and the giant, and a play to destroy the Duke's lands. These make her interpretation stand out among the other versions. There is quite a bit of cruelty in the tale as well, which is unusual for Anna. There is the giant picked apart by birds, the people put on stakes, and the execution of the cook's wife who was apparently innocent. The story resolves with due punishment, but without the added adventures of the hero's journey. It is impossible to tell if Anna's version has always been this short or if it was repurposed from the opening of a longer tale.

The Hungarian language sometimes uses the same word (*herceg*) for a prince (the son of a king) and for a duke (a hereditary title). Since in this case, the White Duke clearly rules the land and is not merely the heir of a king, I used "duke" in my translation. However, if that sounds too foreign for a folktale, "prince" and "princess" would also suffice.

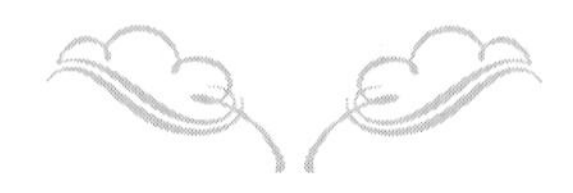

# Golden-Haired Annuska

Once upon a time, there was a great mountain. At the foot of the mountain, there was a thick forest. In the forest, there was a clearing. In the clearing, there was a neat little house – not too big, not too small – just enough for a family. A big family, that is, which included the gamekeeper and his wife, their six children, two grandparents, and a great-grandfather and a great-grandmother. The gamekeeper's name was Mitru János, but everyone called him Faragó (Woodcarver) János because he loved to carve little figurines, horses, dolls, tiny elaborate boxes, crosses, and other things out of wood. His shrewd wife painted them with dyes made of berries, flowers, and bark and she took them to the village where people were always looking to buy such trinkets. Sometimes she even took a bagful of them as far as the city. They earned some extra money this way, and it was much needed. They had many mouths to feed, but only a few hands working.

One day, the wife told János, "I am not going to make it to the village today. I am having pains. You will have to take the merchandise yourself and sell it."

"Fair enough," said her husband. "Just tell me where and how."

"You are not a smart one, are you?" great-grandmother cackled from her bench by the fireplace.

"And you are not exactly the Fairy Queen Ilona either, warming yourself idly all day like that," the gamekeeper grumbled.

The gamekeeper's father told him to quiet down and get going. He would have to stop by at the midwife's house on the way and send her along. She was needed.

As János walked down to the nearby stream, he was greeted by an unusual sight.

A little man was hopping from this side of the water and back, chanting to himself, "I'll be young and I'll be King! I'll be young and I'll be King!"

It looked like he was having such fun that János, who first just laughed at the sight, decided to take a running leap himself… and plopped down straight into the stream! By the time he scrambled out, all the figurines in his bag were worthless, what with the wet dye running and ruining them all. He stared at them crestfallen contemplating what he should do now when the little old man walked up to him.

"Don't worry, my friend, I'll buy them as they are. All of them. I'll make you rich – just promise that you'll give me what you don't know you have at home."

János thought hard about what that could be, but couldn't think of anything he didn't know about, so he agreed. They took the figurines out of the bag, and then the little old man shook his cloak over it and filled it to the brim with shining, ringing golden coins.

"That is enough! I will barely be able to drag it home!" exclaimed János.

"Fair enough. Just don't forget your promise!" and with that, the little man disappeared.

On the way home, János remembered that he was supposed to fetch the midwife. He hid the bag under a bush by the stream, ran to her house, and told her she should hurry. When he returned to the bush, the bag was gone! It had vanished without a trace. No matter how János searched, he could not find a single golden coin. He had to sulk home with his head hanging low.

He cheered up just a little when he was told he had a bouncing baby daughter, but soon he remembered the lost gold again. Even though he knew she wouldn't believe him, he told all to his wife. The wife started to cry. They had the chance to be rich, and now it was gone. She'd rather he had never gone out… to let a chance go like that! Their new baby daughter would have no food, no clothes. But as they looked at the child, they were amazed to see light glinting off her head. Her hair was made of the purest spun gold! It was glowing like the sun. They immediately named her Aranyhajú (Golden-haired) Annuska. The entire family sat around her, petting her golden locks in awe. This was how the midwife found them when she finally arrived. She saw immediately that she had nothing left to do, but, as she looked at the newborn, she almost fainted at how beautiful Annuska looked.

"My word, if the King could see this! He would take her and raise her as a princess, and he would make all of you wealthy!"

Her words rang in the family's ears for a long time. Life went on. Annuska was the heart of the household. She grew like a weed, started talking, and running by the time she turned one. She was so kind and good that all her siblings followed her lead. No one wanted to see her go, so sending her to the King's palace remained a distant possibility they kept putting off. These marvels, all the joy, and all the dreams of wealth and nobility made János completely forget about the promise he had made on the day Annuska was born.

Then, one stormy night, the door banged open and there stood the little old man. At that moment, János remembered his promise. His eyes grew wide in fear. But the next moment he also remembered that the gold was lost, so he could claim that the deal was never completed. As he was searching for words, the little old man walked over to the fireplace to warm himself. The great-grandparents peered out of their cozy corners to marvel at him.

"What do you want from us, little one?" asked great-grandmother cautiously.

"I am here to collect a debt, but it seems the debt is not remembered. I will wait until morning. Then, if I am not paid, I will take my revenge."

*What should I do now?* János racked his brains. *I cannot give up my own child! Not Annuska! We never even got to spend the gold! He has no claim on me.* The little old man saw the struggle on his face, but never said a thing until the next morning.

Then, he stood in front of János and declared, "I will not take your golden-haired daughter. I can see you all love her very much. Give me one of the other six. You have enough to go around."

The wife stared at her husband in horror, not understanding why they would have to give *any* child to the stranger.

But János answered, "I will not give you any of my children! The gold disappeared on the day you gave it to me, while I went to fetch the midwife. It was probably not even real gold. Do not look for a child here. We love them alike and, even if we barely scrape by, we will make ends meet somehow and raise them all."

"Very well," said the little man, "I will leave you for now, but next time, I will not be so kind. And don't send Annuska anywhere, not even to the King's court. If you comb her hair, you'll have a golden coin for every brush. Make sure to do it in secret because if anyone sees you doing it, there will be more trouble."

János was relieved to see the little man go and grateful for the advice. The moment his wife put the girl down, he brushed Annuska's hair once – clink! A gold coin fell out. He did it a second time – clink! Then a third – clink! It worked! He went to the town the next day to buy everything they needed, happily whistling, and hoping for a brighter future. But the Devil never sleeps! While he was away, great-grandmother, who had heard every word the little old man had said, sidled up to Annuska. Even though the girl was wailing, she brushed and brushed and *brushed* until her apron was full of golden coins.

"Where did you get all those coins, great-grandmother?" the wife asked, shocked when she saw the gold.

"There are loads of money under every strand of Annuska's hair. Your simpleton husband just never thought to tell you!"

The great-grandparents then asked János to buy them a new house, and they moved out with all their meager belongings. They lived there, spending the gold, keeping servants and maids, and warming themselves by their own fireplace. In the meantime, there was much distress in the Faragó household. Annuska refused to eat or drink for three days straight. Her mother blamed János, claiming all the brushing had made the child sick. But it wasn't so. What really happened was that Annuska was not to be brushed with people watching, as the little old man had instructed. Great-grandmother had brushed her right outside the house. A wandering apprentice boy had stared at the girl so hard he gave her the evil eye. They had had another child who got the evil eye before, and they smoked him properly, so that the curse went away. But this time, the apprentice had already disappeared. There was no way to undo the curse. Annuska got weaker every day. She was dying.

One morning, the girl asked her parents to take her to the stream as she wanted to look at the water one last time. János picked her up gently and carried her down to the stream. The mother followed, lagging, as she was crying hard. Suddenly, János tripped and fell. He let go of Annuska, and the girl rolled straight into the stream. By the time they ran down to the shore, they could only catch a glimpse of her golden locks disappearing underwater. The mother, screaming, jumped straight after her. As János stared at the waves in horror, the little old man suddenly appeared at his elbow.

"Which would be worse, losing them both or giving me Annuska?"

"Don't torture me, good man, I am losing my mind from grief already!"

"Well, since you called me a good man… I'll tell you this was all a test. Here, take this ladle and pour water from the stream onto the ground."

János poured water twice. Suddenly, there was Annuska and her mother standing on the shore, and they were not even wet! Instead of slimy water, their dresses were covered in gold. See, what really happened was that the bag János hid under a bush all those years ago had been found by a pig who routed the coins into the ground. When the little old man created an illusion, hiding Annuska and her mother in the bush instead of the stream, all the gold stuck to their clothes. Annuska laughed, her eyes bright and her cheeks rosy; the curse of the evil eye was broken.

They walked home carrying the coins. As they counted the coins in the living room, they talked about the little old man. Maybe he was a good soul after all? He had been helping them all along. As they talked, a gorgeous carriage pulled up outside the window and out stepped a handsome young prince.

"You have been talking about me, so here I am! My curse has been broken. I used to be that little old man. Now I am a king restored to my throne, and I live nearby. I would like to marry Annuska, and I promise she will never be far from home. Look!"

They all looked out the window and saw a shining palace just down the road. The Faragó family wanted Annuska to be happy. Once she was old enough to marry, they held a beautiful wedding for her and the King. There was no need to hide her golden hair anymore. Every day, one of her siblings brushed it and collected the coins. They all became wealthy and free to live their own lives. Maybe they are still living happily somewhere today.

**Comments**

This tale opens with a familiar scene: "Child unwittingly promised" (Thompson Motif Index, S242). It is the same motif as the beginning of Grimm's famous *Nixie of the Mill-Pond*, or their *Handless Maiden;* I have also found a Slovakian version that had a golden-haired beauty promised in exchange for riches. In many stories, it leads to the child being given away and raised by some supernatural, and often cruel, entity (the Devil, a dragon, a sorcerer, or a witch). Sometimes the parents try to trick the adversary out of taking their own child, replacing it with others. But in the end, keeping the promise is usually unavoidable (or is avoided at a great cost, as you see in the *Handless Maiden*). Anna, however, once again takes a surprising turn with the story when the "little old man" proves to be capable of empathy and willing to help the poor family. Just like in the tale of *The Cheerful Prince*, the drama mainly revolves around the members of the family and the father's good-natured, yet somewhat forgetful personality.

Brushing gold from one's hair is a motif that can be found all over European folklore, as well as other Hungarian tales. Sometimes flowers, gemstones, or golden roses fall from the locks instead of coins. J.F Campbell, author of *Popular Tales of the West Highlands*, suggested that the image was born from people brushing their hair and seeing sparks in the dark. Whether it is true or not, it remains a very compelling image.

The text of this story was more jumbled than the others in the collection. Sometimes it was hard to understand details, and the teller herself seemed to jump between events and ideas. For example, when the great-grandmother brushed Annuska's hair by force, it was hard to tell whether the entire family moved into a new mansion or just the great-grandparents. It was also hard to pinpoint *whose* parents, grandparents, and great-grandparents made up the little family. I did my best to smooth out these details, but they are up for interpretation.

It is similarly difficult to decide how old Annuska is at any point in the story. When she is cursed by the evil eye, she seems to still be a child; but immediately after her curse is broken, the young King comes and marries her. I added the "old enough to marry" part, but it would also be possible to tell the tale with an adult (by the standards of the time) Annuska suffering from the curse.

The "evil eye" is a strong part of Hungarian folklore and the standard go-to explanation for children's illnesses – even my own grandfather remembers one of his siblings being treated for it. Anyone can give the "evil eye," even unintentionally, if they are observing something not intended for an audience (such as the brushing of Annuska's hair), or if they admire something too long or too hard (and maybe with a hint of jealousy). To cure it, first it had to be decided *who* put the curse on the child (often by magical means), and then a ritual had to be performed – this often involved bathing the victim in water infused with something that had belonged to the culprit (hair, clothing, etc.). Anna mentions that one of Annuska's siblings had been "smoked" and cleansed that way. "Smoking" (which similarly involved the burning of a piece of the culprit's hair or clothes) was also a common part of Hungarian folk medicine until recent times. In this story, since the apprentice walked away and couldn't be found, there was no chance for cleansing Annuska by traditional means.

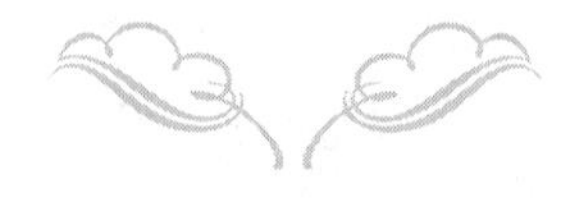

# The Maiden With the Red-Gold Hair

Once upon a time, nobody knows where and nobody knows when, there was a beautiful city ruled by a handsome young king. The city was always buzzing with life because celebrations were held for their beloved ruler – his birthday, his name day, the anniversary of his coronation, and so on. For every celebration, droves of women came to his palace bearing gifts. Some brought a roast pig, some brought a roast capon, and the fancy ones sometimes even brought a roast peacock. Many simply brought large bouquets of fresh flowers or hand-embroidered pieces of clothing. But no matter how they tried to buy his attention, the King pushed all presents aside without a second look and with an exasperated sigh.

The gifts would all have been wasted had it not been for a very clever servant. He made sure that the food was distributed to whomever needed it, and he sold the non-edibles at reasonable prices keeping the King's coffers well-lined with money. Everyone got a favorable deal. The buyers received goods fit for royalty, the court had money to spend, and the servant made sure his beloved King did not have to worry about useless clutter piling up. That is, until the King found out about the servant's clever side job. He kicked his servant out of court for trading his property without permission. The next servant he hired was not so creative.

One day, the beautiful King decided that he wanted to get married as he was getting terribly bored without a wife. The moment word got out, the court filled with an ocean of women: maidens, ladies, peasant girls, and merchants' daughters all dressed in their finest and pouring through the gates, presenting such a colorful sight that even the sun paused in the sky to admire them.

But the King didn't. Whatever they looked like, he always wanted something else. If one was blonde, he wanted a brunette; if one had auburn hair, he wished for a blonde. No lady was good enough, smart enough, or interesting enough. The more the selection dragged out, the more people began to whisper. Finally, a rumor sprang up that if the King could not find a wife within a year, he would never have one. The moment the rumor reached the King's ears, he grew furious. He suspected that one of the ladies was spreading it to scare him into making a hasty choice. Being the stubborn nobleman, he vowed not to decide until the year was up.

What he *did* do, however, was summon a wise woman. The King asked her to gaze into the magic well and tell him who his wife would be. The magic well was the treasure of the town. If someone looked in it, they would glimpse the face of their future spouse – or their own death (whichever would arrive first). Not many people took the chance, which is why the King hired someone else to do it for him.

When the wise old woman arrived to look and reveal the great secret of the future Queen's identity, the King and the woman proceeded to the well with a great crowd trailing behind. The wise woman peered into the depths, and she saw a gorgeous girl. A unique girl who was neither blonde nor brunette, but rather she had hair the color of fire - like molten red-gold. She also had a black mole under her left eye, a beauty mark and the sign of true perfection.

"Tell me, grandmother - what kind of a maiden will I marry?" the King asked.

"A maiden with red-gold hair who has a mole under her left eye, which is the sign of true beauty," the wise woman answered promptly.

She was richly rewarded for her answer.

People were stunned by the news. No one had ever even heard of such a girl! Messengers, servants, and knights were dispatched to search for her everywhere and bring her to the King. But no one could find a maiden (or even a married woman) with red-gold hair. People talked about nothing else in all four corners of the realm.

Eventually, the news about the beautiful King's future wife reached an old Duchess in the neighboring kingdom. She wanted the King to marry her daughter, and she was not afraid to trick him into it. She mixed herbs and potions until she managed to dye the girl's hair a red-gold color, and she faked a beauty mark by painfully stitching a small black bean onto her left cheek. When the messengers stopped at her palace on their way home, she presented her daughter to them. When they asked why she did not show her daughter the first time they visited, she made up a hasty excuse. She claimed she wanted them to see for themselves that there was no *other* girl in the world quite so unique and beautiful. And since the Duchess's daughter was indeed beautiful, the messengers took the happy news to the beautiful King's court.

The King immediately ordered wedding preparations to commence. He sent a great, elaborate carriage to fetch his bride, and he sent out invitations to everyone that mattered. People were looking forward to the celebrations that were to last several days and involve feasts open for everyone, even the poorest beggar. Since there were so many guests on the list, and so many commoners expected, the court needed a large kitchen staff. They hired dozens of helpers, and even sent for more from the neighboring towns. The King had splendid wedding gifts made for his bride, and he displayed them happily in a room for all the guests to see. There were dresses, shoes, necklaces, rings, and all kinds of glittering treasures piled to the ceiling.

One of the kitchen helpers, a female cook, had a daughter. She did not travel with her mother.

When the old woman returned home for the night and told her

about all the beautiful treasures she had seen, the daughter laughed, "I promise you, mother, one day all of those things will be mine."

The mother was stunned and worried her daughter might be losing her mind. However, she told her to come to the wedding the next day anyway to see the beautiful Princess who had hair just like hers and even the same mole under her eye.

But the daughter, with the red-gold hair and the true sign of beauty, didn't go.

The wedding was the most splendid celebration the city had ever seen. Everyone was happy, everyone except for the new Queen. There was not even a smile on her lips. After dinner, her husband took her by the hand and led her to the room full of gifts. He was sure that it would cheer her and make her laugh, but all he got was a wavering smile. The King embraced his wife and caressed her cheek to show how much he loved her already, but the moment he touched her face, she screamed. No wonder she did! The black bean stitched under her skin hurt so much it was driving her insane. She could not tell the King that, and he decided not to touch her anymore as he was worried that she might be having sunstroke or some other condition. The wedding celebrations ended. People returned to their homes, still discussing the details of the feast and the entertainment, how beautiful the Queen was, and how much the King obviously loved her already. No one noticed that he was being tricked or that the new wife felt utterly miserable.

Time passed. The red-gold dye began to fade away from the Queen's hair. Even worse, the beauty mark began to swell and grow. One morning, out popped a bean sprout right on the Queen's cheek! This swayed the King a little, but she was still his wife in the eyes of God. He decided not to make a fuss and simply cut off the sprout. There was no way a queen could go around with beans growing on her face, after all! He called in his trusted chariot driver first, but the man refused to cut the sprout worried he might injure the Queen's face. Next, he called in the barber who did not hesitate much. Instead of cutting off the sprout, he nicked the skin itself and out popped the whole black bean. The pain was finally gone from the Queen's cheek, but the King was growing suspicious.

"Tell me, my dear wife, how come you had a bean growing on your cheek? And how come your hair is not as bright red-gold as it was when we first met?"

The poor Queen broke down crying and confessed everything. She told the King how she never had red-gold hair and never had a beauty mark under her eye. It was because of her mother who wanted her to marry a king that she dyed her hair and stitched the bean into her cheek. But now that it had grown out and the dye was fading, she was tired of lying. Her mother had warned her not to say anything, even if it hurt, because she would never take back her daughter, the King would chase her away, and she had nowhere else to go. Words came pouring out, and so did tears.

The King was stunned. He knew now that his marriage was based on a lie, but what could he do? To tell the truth, he had never been in love with the girl, despite the prophecy, but now he felt tremendous pity as well. He decided to allow her to keep living in the castle.

More time passed. One day the Queen was in town when she saw the cook's daughter, the one that had *real* red-gold hair and a *real* beauty mark. The daughter had not gone to the wedding, but she was in the city now going about errands. The Queen took one look, turned around, went straight home, and got so sick with worry and fear that she never left her bed. She was fading away fast with distress, and in her fever, she called for her mother. The King finally sent for the Duchess. He was angry at her for the trick she had played, but not at his wife. Since the sick woman wanted her mother, he allowed her to come; the King was a good man at heart. When the Duchess came and saw her daughter, she began to scold her and berate her, calling her useless and disappointing. The Queen said nothing. She just lay in bed and cried. From then on, she became worse every day from her mother's words as much as the illness. The King sent for the female cook to make her famous, rich broth for his suffering wife.

Before the woman left for the castle, her daughter gave her a strand of her red-gold hair. She told her mother that if she put that in the broth, the Queen would be cured. But in the end, it was not the ill woman who found the hair – it was the King himself.

At first, he wanted to yell at the servants. Whose hair had made its way into his wife's broth, and who was responsible for such a disgrace?! But when he saw the glint of red gold, he became intrigued. *What a marvel*, he thought. He put the strand of hair away. The next day, he served the broth himself and, indeed, there was another glimmer of golden hair in it. This continued for three days.

Soon after, the Queen died. She was buried with great pomp and honor, surrounded by such a sea of flowers that their scent made people dizzy. But what made them reel even more, was one of the maidens who came to the funeral and stood in the back with the commoners. She had true red-gold hair and a beauty mark under her left eye. Everyone stared at her, except for the King, who was too bereaved and too miserable to notice any woman at the funeral of his wife.

But somebody else did notice - the clever servant. Even though the King had exiled him for selling gifts, the servant still cared for his former master, and he did not want him to miss out on happiness the second time around. He could see that this girl was a genuine beauty as the magic well had foretold. When people dispersed after the funeral, he secretly followed her to the neighboring town and noted the house to which she returned.

After three days, the King took the three strands of red-gold hair, gathered his advisors, and asked for their opinion.

"What should be done if my late wife was not the true bride?"

It was them, after all, who had brought the girl to him. He assured the terrified advisors that he wasn't angry – she had been a good wife and kind, but now she was dead and buried. He did not send her away while she lived, and she had died a queen. The one that deserved punishment was the old Duchess for causing so much misery with her intrigue.

They gathered the great council. The Duchess was also invited. She had to vote on what the punishment should be for someone who would cheat the King out of his happiness and cause the death of an innocent woman. Everyone suggested options, but the cruelest came from the Duchess herself. She did not suspect a thing because she thought her secret was safe in the grave with her daughter. She suggested that such a criminal should be sewn into an ox hide. Everyone agreed, and made a clamor for the punishment to be carried out immediately. The Duchess realized too late that she had sentenced herself. They immediately killed and skinned a large ox and sewed the old woman into its hide. As the wet hide dried, it shrank. The Duchess suffocated inside it. This was her punishment for cheating two people out of their happiness.

In the meantime, the maiden with the red-gold hair prepared herself for a visit from the King. She was a clever girl, and she knew her time was near. Once all was said and done, and the mourning days ended, the loyal servant went to the advisors and told them about the real bride hidden in a cook's house. The message was passed on to the King himself, who at first did not want to believe that such luck was possible and demanded to know how they found a girl so close by after so long. The advisors hemmed and hawed and finally confessed that the exiled servant had brought them the news.

Things happened fast from that moment on. The King summoned the clever servant, and after a long talk and some apologies on both sides, invited him back to court as his personal advisor – if what he claimed was true. They rode straight to the cook's house where the girl greeted them in the doorway with a smile, red-gold hair shining in the sun. When the two young people, who were meant for each other, met for the very first time, the King was so overjoyed he did not even care that her mother was only a cook. He proposed straight away, and she accepted without hesitation. There was a second wedding, even more splendid than the first. The feast was even better since the bride's mother made all the best delicacies, spiced with pride and joy.

The young couple visited the first Queen's grave on their wedding day bringing an armful of fresh flowers. As the handsome King and his beautiful, red-gold haired wife stood in the churchyard, they were such a sight that even the sun paused in the sky to look. They were so beautiful that people wept with joy. Even the clever servant, standing to the side, wiped away a tear or two from the corners of his eyes. Or at least this is how my grandmother told me, and this is how I am telling it to you.

**Comments**

I have never heard another "False Bride" (ATU 403) story where the false bride was treated with so much kindness. I especially love the closing scene of the tale where the King and the true Queen visit the false bride's grave with flowers. Even though the original text was a little jumbled, I am surprised that this tale was not included in any of the collections showcasing Anna's stories. It is one of my favorites. Since we find out that she learned it from her grandmother, I have always wondered if the small moments of empathy were handed down in the family tradition, from one remarkable woman to the other, or if they were Anna's own inventions.

In the Archives, this story was titled, "The duchess sewn into an ox hide," but I thought that it was unfortunate to highlight the darkest part of the tale instead of its most appealing visual image (the girl's red-gold hair). Since folktales don't usually have titles in the oral tradition, I decided to replace it. Once again, the punishment for evil is quite graphic, a sentence the cruel mother brings upon her own head (it is a common motif in Hungarian folktales to ask the unsuspecting villain to suggest their own means of execution). While not every audience is prepared to deal with the gory details, slow suffocation is an interesting parallel for the mother's abusive practices towards her long-suffering daughter.

I have also been amused by the opening anecdote about the King's clever servant. Anna enjoys elaborating small elements of her stories (i.e. women's admiration for their prince) into longer, practical narratives ("what to do with all the gifts?"). When I began working with this tale, I really wanted to see the clever servant return later in the story to save the day somehow – but he never did. So, I tweaked the ending a little and brought the servant back instead of some nameless, character-less advisor.

Once again, I had to make a choice regarding the translation of *herceg*. I decided to go with "king" instead of "prince" or "duke" this time as it seemed to fit the love story better. It also gives an extra layer of motivation for the Duchess, so desperate to marry her daughter "up" into royalty. The beauty mark on the girl's cheek is supposedly the sign of *hétszépség*, "beauty seven times" – the greatest beauty in the world. The King calls the chariot driver to cut out his wife's bean sprout first; chariot drivers were also responsible for the horses and, therefore, adept in simple healing procedures. In the end, it is the barber (known for providing medical services such as bloodletting) that completes the task.

Recognizing a lost bride or finding a worthy wife by a stray strand of golden hair is not uncommon in Western tales. The most famous example is probably the romance of *Tristan and Iseult*. In this case, the clever girl, biding her time, uses it as a hint for the King. She nudges him in the right direction with a literal glimmer of hope, instead of busting in through the door causing more harm than good. The girl's intelligence and calculated patience makes her an interesting character in this tale.

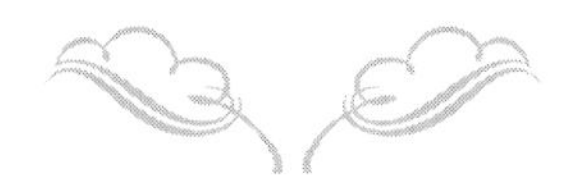

# Jancsi Goes to the Glass Mountain

Once upon a time, there was a poor woman who spent her days crying. She had good reason because when her husband was not getting into a fight, recovering from a fight or threatening to fight someone, then her son Jancsi was following in his father's footsteps by being the center of every brawl in town. One day, Jancsi got into such a fight that he broke all the windows in the tavern and had no money to pay for the glass. The poor woman went to the judge asking what she could do about the debt weighing on them.

"Let both men go to jail and think about what they have done," suggested the judge.

But that was easier said than done because the poor woman had no sway over the two big, strong men, and she also loved them too much to let them go to jail. So, she didn't say a word and waited. Soon after her husband fell into bed, and he groaned so miserably that even the Devil would have felt pity for him. Before she could ask what was wrong, he rolled over and died. This scared their son. Jancsi realized he'd have to change his ways before it was too late.

After the funeral, the lad set out for town to look for service so that he could pay for the glass windows and earn money for his mother. On the road, he met a stranger who gave him different advice.

"Why would you work like an ox when you could go to the Glass Mountain and bring enough glass for *all* the houses in town?" asked the stranger.

Jancsi thought this was a brilliant suggestion. He would pay his debt to the tavern and maybe even sell the extra glass and become rich! It sounded like a comfortable business. He set out for the Glass Mountain immediately. But it was not as near as he'd thought; there was yet much struggle and many tears between Jancsi and his goal.

His mother, when he did not come back home, thought that he'd gotten in a fight again. The longer he was missing, the surer she was that he'd been killed. As time passed, she slowly forgot about her grief and went about her life alone, remembering her son as the nice boy he never was.

Jancsi walked and walked and walked. When he ran out of food and clothing, he stopped and worked as a shepherd for a while and then he moved on. He traveled so far that he was sure he'd reach the edge of the world soon. Then one night, he came across a small cottage with light pouring from the windows.

It was the house of the Grandmother of Darkness. When she opened the door to his knock, Jancsi almost fainted. She had a nose that reached all the way to the ground! She leaned on it, using the appendage as a walking stick. Jancsi stared for a few heartbeats, but he soon gathered himself and greeted her politely.

"Good evening to you, dear grandmother!"

"Good of you to call me grandmother," she growled. "Otherwise, I would have fed your blood to the dogs! What are you doing here, where even the sun only visits on occasion?

"I am seeking service, grandmother."

"You are in luck, then. The Devil took my servant, just the other day, to mind the fires of Hell. You can be my new servant. How would you like that, hmm?"

Jancsi was shocked when he saw what his job would be. He had to keep a giant oven burning with wood that was being hauled in from the forest by devils. They were swarming with such speed that they almost knocked him off his feet. *This is not a place for a mortal man*, he thought, *I'd better get out of here fast*.

The old hag must have guessed his thoughts because she spoke up, "Don't worry about running away. I will only keep you a short time. If you serve me well, I'll reward you in the end."

Jancsi agreed to the terms, but he was still curious what the oven was for, what were they baking, and for whom were they baking? The oven seemed large enough to supply bread for an entire army, but he had seen no army or city nearby.

The hag must have guessed these thoughts, too, because she warned him, "Don't be too curious, Jancsi; it will make you old before your time. I used to be curious, too, and now look at me! Everything is as it should be. Don't you mind that, just do your job as I say. And be careful what you think because I know your thoughts as well."

Back in those days, three days made a whole year. The devils hauled the firewood without a pause. Jancsi minded the oven, keeping the flames burning evenly until the three days were done as was his service with them. At the end of the third day, the hag appeared again.

"You have served me well. Ask whatever you wish for as payment, and I'll give it to you. But be warned, never talk about what you have seen here or you will be sorry!"

Jancsi was surprised. He had not seen anything unusual - other than the giant oven and the devils bringing firewood, of course. But now he was *really* curious. He decided to spend the last night finding out the truth. He started with feeding his dinner to a large cat, so that a full stomach would not make him drowsy. As soon as the meal was finished, he watched the cat keel over and die. *Look at that*, he thought. *The old woman had no intention of letting me go alive*. He pretended to go to sleep and waited.

Suddenly he heard carriages pulling up outside the house, so many of them that the walls shook from the rattle of their wheels. It sounded like several people were tossing sacks of grain off the carriages, hundreds and hundreds of them, without an end. Jancsi peered out the window, and his blood froze. The things being tossed from the carriages were not sacks, but corpses. Human corpses. He had no way of telling where they came from, but they were corpses for sure, and they were being tossed straight into the oven. The devils took care that they were not burned too much. When they were good and roasted, they put them back on the carriages, and they all drove away.

As Jancsi was watching in horror, he noticed that someone was waving at him through the window. He snuck out of the house and went around the corner to find himself face to face with a beautiful girl.

"I know who you are and what you came here for, but I have to warn you. In the morning, when my mother asks you what you want, don't ask for anything or you'll end up like all those people. Ask her to show you the way to the Glass Mountain. Tell her you want no other payment for your work. If you do so, we'll see each other again. If you don't, you'll never see me, or your mother, or anyone… for you will be dead."

Jancsi had to scratch his ears to make sure he was awake, but in that moment, he heard the hag's screeching voice from the house.

"Wake up, wake up, Jancsi, and come on in so we can settle your payment!"

Jancsi pretended not to know a thing as he went inside. When the hag asked him what he wanted, he politely asked her to show him the way to the Glass Mountain. The hag got furious. How could she show him the way? She could barely walk! And besides, she'd never go there anyway because her oldest enemy, Sunlight, lived right there on the mountain.

"Well, then don't give me anything. I'll go alone," Jancsi retorted.

"My daughter must have talked to you, she is smart like that," the hag grumbled. "I'll walk you a little way and point you in the right direction because I don't want to be in your debt. You will not have it this easy when you come to the Glass Mountain because my mother lives there, too. See if you can cheat her like you cheated me!"

*Very well*, thought Jancsi. *I have gotten this far; maybe God will help me along the way.* As they stepped out onto the road, the hag grabbed her own nose and twisted it. The next moment, they were standing at the bottom of the Glass Mountain. Jancsi stared, bewildered, and the Grandmother of Darkness gave a cackle.

"Are you marveling at my nose? I can turn it into many things. It can be a carriage that flies or a magic horse that takes us anywhere faster than thought. It can even be a stick that beats anyone I want. Now you know enough not to ask more. This is where I leave you. See how you fare on your own."

With that, she disappeared without a trace. Jancsi wondered if she had been swallowed up by the earth or dissolved into the night, not that he minded that she was gone. As he looked around, he saw another cottage very much like the one he had just served in. Beyond the cottage rose the Glass Mountain, glittering in the sun. *Almost there*, he thought, not knowing that he would still suffer a great deal before making it to the top.

As he stood looking around, another old hag poked her head out of the cottage. She was seven times uglier than the previous one, with a wart on her nose so big she could barely peer around it.

"Hey, young man! Why are you standing around, while everyone else is busy picking apples on the mountain?"

At the mention of apples, Jancsi cheered up. He had not seen an apple since he'd left home. He walked up to the cottage and greeted the old woman politely.

"Good evening to you, dear grandmother!"

"If it is so good, you can keep it," she grumbled. "You may stay as my servant, if you want. The previous one had been sucked up into the Moon last night."

*What a strange place. The Moon comes here for drinks?* wondered Jancsi, but he agreed to the service nonetheless. One year, made of three days, was no big deal to him.

"What will be my job?"

"Not much, really – you only have to guard the apple orchard. You can even eat one apple every day. Just make sure you don't pick one of the small ones."

*I like this a lot better than the last place*, thought Jancsi. *She even wants me to eat the bigger apples!* He went straight to the orchard at the foot of the mountain and marveled at how beautiful, how luscious all the apples looked. Eventually, he walked up to one of the trees and reached out to pick a pretty, red apple to eat. But the moment he touched it, there was a terrible, whining scream as if a hundred babies had been thrown into fire. He looked around, startled, looking for its source. He let go of the apple and examined the trees closer – they all looked rather strange. Almost shaped like… people? He spent the entire day wandering around, looking at them. He only returned to the cottage after dark.

"How was your day, Jancsi, my son? Were you not hungry for any apples?"

Jancsi had learned from his last service, and lied without batting an eye.

"Not at all, grandmother. I was already full of their delicious scent."

"Very well, then. Keep up the good work, and I will treat you well. But beware, I can't go into the orchard, but I can see you from here."

The next morning Jancsi went into the garden again, and he marveled at the apples until he found one he wanted. But as soon as he reached out to pluck it, the apple smacked him on the hand so hard he staggered back and fell to the ground. He only woke up at nightfall. Back in the cottage, the hag asked him again.

"How was your day? Did you eat one?"

"I did, grandmother," Jancsi lied.

The next day he went to the orchard again. He wanted to figure out what kind of strange apples grew in it and from where they had come. He even climbed a tree. It groaned under him, almost like a person, every time he stepped on a branch or snapped a twig. Jancsi was perplexed, and found nothing at the top. At last, as he climbed down, an apple fell into his lap. It was a shining, bright red fruit, and he picked it up for a bite. In that moment, instead of an apple, the beautiful girl sprung up from his lap, the same one he had met at the other cottage.

"Jancsi, my dear, you have almost broken the curse on me and on many others. But you must keep your wits about you now. Tonight, when your service is up, do not eat anything just like last time or you'll die. But when my grandmother asks you tomorrow what you want as payment, ask for the crooked stick that is propped up by the door. She won't be keen on giving it, but insist anyway. Then climb the Glass Mountain. I will meet you there."

Everything happened as she said. Jancsi went home that night, and he told the hag all about how nicely the trees danced and how sweet the apples smelled. He had not even been hungry all day.

*You were not, because you could not eat*, thought the hag, but aloud she only said, "Here is your dinner. I will pay you tomorrow morning, and you can go wherever you want."

Jancsi pretended to knock the plate off the table. All the food fell to the floor where a large dog ate it and instantly keeled over, dead. The hag was furious that her plan for killing the boy failed. Jancsi went to bed and pretended to sleep. At night, peering out the window, he saw all the apples turn into people, stand begging at the hag's door and asking her to let them live a little longer on earth. She never answered; she slept deeply like a child. With the first light of the morning, the cries subsided. There was nothing left in the garden but twisted apple trees with shining, sweet-scented fruit.

In the morning, the hag asked Jancsi what he wanted as payment for his service. When he asked for the crooked stick, she was astonished. Who could have told him about it? How did he know? He certainly knew more than she had expected, but there was no going back on her word now. She had to give Jancsi the stick. She made him promise not to talk about anything he had seen, and the boy promised, hoping to get away alive. He took the stick, and set out or rather, the stick set out, dragging him along at breakneck speed. It was still morning when they arrived at a pretty, little castle on the top of the Glass Mountain. *I'll serve here and earn enough glass to settle my debt,* Jancsi thought cheerfully, *and maybe take some for my mother as well.*

As soon as he decided, a window opened and out leaned the beautiful girl he had met twice before. She beckoned to him.

"Jancsi, my dear, you are just in time! Today is the last day of my curse. You started to break it when you served my mother and my grandmother. Had you not done it so well or had you eaten their food, I would have died as well as many other people. You have one more task to fulfill, but it won't be hard. Do exactly as you are told. I'll be right beside you the entire time."

As soon as she said that, the gates of the castle opened. Out came another old woman – this one was not ugly like the ones before, just old, and even her speech was different.

"If you wish to stay here, Jancsi, then today you must cross that pond by the castle and catch a fish for my sick great-granddaughter's lunch."

*That shouldn't be so hard,* Jancsi thought – but he was sorely mistaken. There was not a single fish to be found in the entire pond. Hours passed, and lunchtime was drawing near, and yet there was no movement to be seen under the crystal, clear waves. As he floated to the middle of the lake and peered into the water, he suddenly noticed the beautiful girl lying at the bottom. The morning was almost over, and he had no fish. He thought that maybe one was hiding under her, so he jumped out of the boat, waded into the water, and turned her over. She instantly disappeared, but droves of fish sprang free from under her. He caught the largest and prettiest one and carried it home strung on a willow switch. The old woman greeted him happily and put the fish straight into the pan. As they sat down to eat at noon, the beautiful girl joined them at the table with a brilliant smile. The old woman offered some fish to Jancsi, but he refused. He did not know it, but by doing so, he saved himself, the girl, and many others.

The same thing happened for three days in a row. One night, as Jancsi sat in the garden, he saw the beautiful girl walking along, hand in hand with a handsome man. His heart ached. Had she been lying to him? Leading him on? Who was that handsome lord? A suitor? Another traveler? He did not have to wait long to find out. The girl noticed him brooding nearby and introduced them to each other. The lord turned out to be her brother, cursed like everyone else on the Glass Mountain.

When the year of service ended, the old woman asked Jancsi what he wanted as payment. But he had not had a chance to get the girl's advice on the matter yet, so he asked for some time to think. He remembered not to eat dinner. He knocked the plate over and watched as a cat ate all the food, but the cat did not die. In fact, it rubbed against his leg purring, and spoke like a person.

"You have fed me well, Jancsi, so I will help you. If the old woman asks you what you want, ask for the small wooden bowl from the pantry. When you have it, take it out to the courtyard, and smash it to as many pieces as you can."

So, he did. The old woman did not want to give him the bowl at first. She promised to give him glass instead, as much as he wanted, enough to make him rich, telling him he'd be the laugh of the town if he returned home with just a measly wooden bowl to show for all his troubles. But Jancsi insisted and as soon as she reluctantly handed over the bowl, he took it outside and chopped it into fine woodchips. When he looked up, he was stunned to see a crowd of people around him – all the souls that had been imprisoned in the bowl by the three hags. Out of the crowd stepped two beautiful figures, the girl and her brother. The Prince thanked him, and the Princess hugged him, laughing and crying.

"Jancsi, my dear, I am yours and you are mine, from now until forever. My brother and all these people are yours to rule for you have saved us all."

All Jancsi could think of was that he was now a wealthy man. If he wanted, he could have this entire mountain taken home to his town and give new windows to everyone. He could make sure his mother was not poor anymore, but lived comfortably to the end of her days. With that in mind, he turned to the Princess:

"I love you, and I want to marry you, but you have to come home with me to my mother first. I am afraid it is very far away."

"Not for us, love," she smiled. "There are all kinds of wise people here. If you wish to go, there is one that can take us there in the blink of an eye. All of them await your command. And I am happy to be your loyal wife."

They held their wedding on that very same day. It was a wonderful celebration with many treats and delicacies. The next morning, they got into a carriage. Before Jancsi sighed once, thanking God for all his good fortune, they were already at his mother's door. She was as happy as a mother could be, but looked a lot older. Jancsi, too, noticed in that moment that time had not passed him by either. The hair at his own temples was turning grey. He paid all his debts in town, with interest and apologies. Then he built a large stone house for his family, and they lived there in wealth and prosperity for the rest of their days.

If you don't believe me, go to the Glass Mountain. The people Jancsi saved from the curse still live there to this very day.

**Comments**

This story is so rich in symbols and imagery that it would merit its own book. It is one of the most "mythical" tales of Anna's repertoire. It is a classic journey from the Grandmother of Darkness to Sunlight at the top of the Glass Mountain, from desperation to salvation. It has a distinct feel of Dante's *Inferno* about it, with the bodies of dead people being roasted and souls turned into trees begging for relief. It is not the only tale in Anna's repertoire that involves humans being turned into apples, even though that motif is not very common in the Hungarian tradition. The Glass Mountain, on the other hand, is well known all over Europe (Thompson Motif Index, F751). It is often used in the opening formula of Hungarian folktales to signal distance: *"Once upon a time, beyond the*

*Óperenciás Sea, beyond the Glass Mountain...* " It is, literally, the edge of the world. Anna's practical thinking shows when the hero of the tale considers how much money he could make from providing glass windows for his entire town.

There were a few confusions in this story that I had to untangle. One was that Jancsi was asked to bring fish for lunch, but then he only came home at night for dinner. Choosing between options, I chose lunch and sent him home by midday, partly because lunch is the main meal in Hungary, and partly because I suspect the beautiful girl had something to do with the sun shining at noon above the mountains.

Another confusion occurred around the figures of the three witches. The first one is the Grandmother of Darkness; the other two are unnamed. We find out that one is the mother of the first, and the beautiful maiden is also daughter to the one in the castle, and sister to the Grandmother of Darkness – except the maiden also calls the Grandmother of Darkness her mother the first time she appears to Jancsi. To hammer out the family tree a little, I made them into consecutive generations, with the maiden as the youngest, and the old woman in the castle the oldest. The identity of the "Sunlight" that the Grandmother of Darkness is so afraid of is unsure. It could be the girl, the lady of the castle or simply light itself. In my head, she's the girl.

Jancsi is a nickname for János (John). The mention of being "sucked up into the Moon" refers to the folk belief that rainbows arch down to earth to drink water and sometimes accidentally suck animals or people up into the sky, some of whom find a new home in the Moon (in the form of darker spots). The mention of "wise men" with supernatural powers at the end of the story is my translation for the *tudó(s)* ("knowers"), people with extraordinary wisdom and/or abilities in the folk tradition.

# Part Two

## The Kind and the Unkind

"There is no difference between people except between the kind and the unkind," says Anna with a heroine's voice. For this chapter, I selected tales where the central motif, the heroes' most important feature, is kindness, caring, or empathy. While Anna infused many of her stories with the importance of these traits, some stand out from among the hundred with the clarity of their message and the strength of the emotions they evoke. Characters in these tales, while surrounded by magic, experience great human misery and great joy, and the storyteller takes her time describing both. Magic, for once, takes a secondary role to reality. I arranged these six stories in an order that gradually moves from everyday life towards the supernatural and the almost-mythical.

Most of the stories in this chapter are also unique because they, like the majority of Anna's repertoire, do not belong to any recognized folktale type. They seem to have been constructed from the symbols and elements of the folktales she grew up hearing, but it is impossible to tell whether they belong to oral traditions that have since been lost or if they are the product of the incredible creativity and vivid imagination of a single gifted storyteller. Either way, they deserve to be passed on.

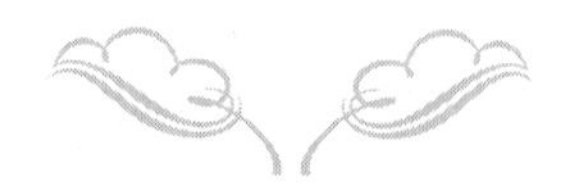

# The Sleepy Lady

Once upon a time, there was a poor woman who had two daughters. Every day they went together to the forest to gather berries, mushrooms, and herbs. The mother knew the uses of all the plants and flowers so, under her direction, the daughters picked them, sorted them, and sold them in town. Everyone knew them for their vast knowledge and expertise, and the mother and her daughters managed to make a living from it.

One day, the daughter of the town judge came down with a very strange illness. She had no fever or pain, and yet, she slept day and night. No doctor could cure her; no entertainment could keep her awake. The judge heard of the woman and her daughters, wise in the ways of herbs, so he sent for them asking for a refreshing potion that would keep the girl awake. The mother brought herbs and made tea, but the tea did not cure the Sleepy Lady. Therefore, she never got payment for her work. The judge was too frustrated and desperate to pay attention to common decency or courtesy. Regardless, the poor woman kept coming back and so did her daughters. They felt sorry for the girl who would fall asleep between question and answer and passed most of her days slumbering.

One day, as they were in the forest picking herbs, the younger daughter came across a strange flower. It had a strong, straight stalk and a scent that you could smell from yards away. She reached out to break it off thinking that such a strong, fresh smell was bound to keep the Sleepy Lady awake - but the flower spoke:

"I know where you want to take me, little girl, but please don't break my stalk! It will only end my life, and my scent will falter. Here, take these two seeds instead."

The flower shook itself, dropping two seeds into the girl's palm.

"Tell the judge's daughter to plant them. If she can watch and wait until they bloom, she will be cured. She will have to keep watch and not fall asleep, even if she must prop her eyelids up! Make sure to tell her that. She can only sleep at night, but must keep watch all day from sunrise to sunset. Otherwise, the seeds won't take root."

The girl brought the seeds to the judge's daughter happily. They planted them together, covered them with soft dirt, and the Sleepy Lady sat down, determined to guard them. However, it wasn't even noon yet, when she had already slumped over and fallen asleep right there in the flowerbed. The poor girl returned to the flower in the forest and told it that they failed.

"Go back to her today," the flower suggested, "and tell her she *has* to do it. She must stay awake and keep watch until the flowers bloom or things will not end well for her."

The next day, the girl told the Sleepy Lady what the flower had said. Her father insisted that she should try again, even if he had to hold her eyes open. The mother and her two daughters believed so strongly that this would cure her, they simply had to try. The judge put two matchsticks into the eyes of the girl, propping up her eyelids. She lasted until the early afternoon, but then she fell asleep with her eyes propped open.

"Make sure she stays awake," the flower told the youngest girl when she returned crying. "If she does not keep watch, she will turn into a flower like me. That will be her fate. Keep her awake."

Everyone was intent on helping the Sleepy Lady. She wished she could have been like other people, only sleeping at night. She was a grown woman, after all, not some infant that needed to sleep during the day. She was beginning to give up hope, thinking that things would never change for her even though her father and the poor family were all trying to help. The youngest girl went back to the flower again, asking what would grow from those magical seeds.

"Nothing," the flower answered simply, "but if she can keep watch for three days without falling asleep, she will be cured."

They went back to the judge and told him that they would guard his daughter for three days, and they would do everything within their power to keep her awake. The judge, eager to see his daughter cured, promised them rich rewards if they completed their task.

The mother was the first to guard the girl. She spent the entire day telling stories, one after another – stories that were so thrilling that the girl forced herself to stay awake and listen to all of them. She did not fall asleep until the evening. Then she tumbled into bed exhausted and slept sweetly until the next day.

When she woke up in the morning, the elder daughter was already waiting for her. She spent the day teaching songs to the Sleepy Lady, singing together with her, making her repeat all verses line by line. One song followed another, and the judge's daughter stayed awake until the last song. It was one about the moonlight, which faded on the poor girl's lips into the dusk. She was exhausted, but another day had passed successfully.

The third morning the younger daughter came with a basket full of snail shells, pebbles, and other shiny things. She poured them at the feet of the Sleepy Lady. They spent the entire day playing, making patterns and pictures out of them. The judge's daughter did not even notice the passage of time until the sun began to set. As evening came, the father and the two girls celebrated together.

"I will never be able to thank you for what you have done for me," said the Sleepy Lady who was not sleepy anymore. Holding the poor girl's hands in hers, she continued, "I will tell you about a dream I had.

Maybe it will bring you luck. I dreamed that the flower, which gave you those seeds, hides a great treasure. You will find your wealth under it if you dig straight down. I know my father promised you a reward, but even with that, I'll never be able to repay your kindness. Therefore, I am telling this dream to you and no one else."

The girl went home and told her mother and sister what the judge's daughter had said.

"Let's try," said the mother, and they went out to the forest together to find the flower.

They brought a shovel, a hoe, and a basket to bring home whatever they should find. But when they dug around the flower and carefully pulled it out, they were disappointed. There was only a large rock under it.

"That was not worth the trouble," grumbled the mother and the older sister.

But the younger one wrapped the rock in a piece of cloth anyway, placed it in the basket along with the uprooted flower, and carried them both home.

That evening, when the family went to bed and put out the lights, they could not go to sleep for the cottage was filled with some strange, clear radiance, so bright that they could have found a needle on the floor. They thought it might be the moonlight at first, but the sky was pitch dark, and the curtains were drawn. The youngest daughter finally noticed that the source of the light was the rock she'd brought home. She covered it with a shawl; darkness enveloped the room.

In the morning, she took the rock out and looked at it closely. She could tell it was not like other rocks. She told her mother they should take it to town and sell it to make their fortune.

"What foolishness is this? Who would buy a rock for enough money to make a family wealthy?" asked her mother.

The younger girl insisted, so the next day they took the rock to a shop in town, a shop that sold all kinds of colorful stones. As it turned out, none of the stones in the shop were quite like theirs. When the shopkeeper saw their diamond (because that's what it was, a diamond as large as a fist), he almost fainted. Where could they have stolen it from? Even the Chinese Emperor did not have gems like this one! The shopkeeper concluded then that they could not have stolen it, and he decided to make a deal.

"Look, good woman, I can't buy this stone. Even if I had three shops full of gems, they would not be enough payment for it. What I can give you is a hundred golden coins now, and the rest when I have sold it. You can buy your own house, the best one in town. You and your daughters will still have money left over to live comfortably until the end of your days."

The girl was happy she'd picked up the stone. Her mother cried tears of joy over the end of their poverty. They went to the judge's daughter to thank her for the gift of her dream. They were given a warm greeting. The Sleepy Lady had not been sleeping during the day ever since they had cured her. She loved the poor woman and her daughters so much that she asked her father if they could be together forever. The judge, who was not opposed to this idea at all, married the woman, and the three girls lived like sisters from that day on. They sang together, played together, danced together, and planted a garden with the strange forest flower in the center of it, beloved and admired (even though it never spoke again). The girls lived together until all three were married and remained close friends even after that. I am sure they still are today.

**Comments**

Some folktale elements are recognizable in this story, even if the tale in its entirety is unique. The challenge to keep the girl awake is like those princesses in fairy tales that either never laugh or never smile until the right suitor comes along. However, in this case, she is cured by friendship, female companionship, and sisterhood rather than romantic love. The rock that turns out to be a diamond also appears in other Hungarian folktales and lights up the room at night, signaling it has special value to poor people who have never seen a gemstone.

The talking flower is the only magical element in the story, and even that one is ambiguous. The seeds turn out to be no more than a trick to keep the girl awake ("watching the grass grow"), and we never find out whether the flower was really a person before or if the warning was an empty threat to motivate the Sleepy Lady. In a later chapter, we will encounter a similar flower (*Touch-me-not*) and learn how she came to be. Anna apparently had a soft spot for talking flora.

The story originally opens with "there was a poor woman who had three daughters." One daughter gets left behind in the story somehow. By the time it comes to keeping the Sleepy Lady awake for three days, there are only two of them. I assume this is because the first day was taken by the mother and her stories. Since I like that image of her, and it gave her even more of a personality (besides being a healer), I decided to cut the number of daughters down to two. The structure of repeating things three times, so common in Hungarian folktales, remains intact regardless. The following story has a similar structure, but with the participation of all three daughters included.

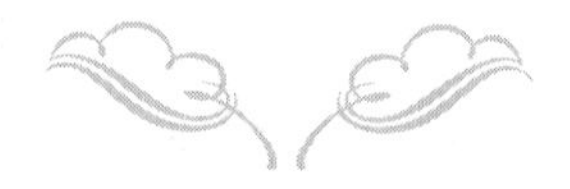

# The Poor Man and the Three Ladies

Once upon a time, there was a wealthy city so clean and so beautiful that it glimmered in the sun. The city had a Captain whose wife loved people so much she always put in a good word for them when they got into trouble – and trouble happened easily, even in a great city like that.

One day, it happened to a poor man whose cows wandered onto someone else's property. They trampled and ruined everything; they did a great deal of damage by treating the neighbor's garden as their pasture. It was an expensive business. The owner of the cows had to pay a high fine to get his livestock back. How could a poor man get enough money for that? When his wife learned that their cows had wandered onto forbidden land and then had been taken to the barn for seized animals, she ran crying to her husband who was doing work in the Captain's gardens at the time. The crying alerted the three mistresses, the daughters of the Captain, and they overheard what the woman was telling her husband about the trouble that had befallen them. They immediately ran to their mother, telling her that a poor family needed help. The lady of the house hurried down to the garden to talk to the couple and to ask them questions: How did they live? Did they have many children? Many livestock? And so on. Her eyes grew wide, however, when the poor man broke down crying.

"We do not have a single child, my lady, although we have had many babies. The moment they are born, the Devil takes them away - every time. My wife tells me that if she has a new one coming, she will jump in the well because she cannot bear the grief anymore. And now they are taking our two little cows away because they wandered into a garden that belongs to the city, and I can't earn enough to pay the fines. Now we have no cows and no future. This is the end of it all. After I am done with my work here, I will go home, and we will both end our lives, give our souls… and our cows… to those who can take better care of them."

"I can see you are in deep grief," said the Captain's wife gently. "Did you have no one to sit at your wife's side when she gave birth? To pray the Devil away?"

The poor man only shook his head in despair. "Who would care for people like us?"

The Captain's wife planted her hands on her hips.

"Don't you fret about the cows. I will take care of that matter. Go home now in peace. When your wife is with child again, you let me know, hear me? I have three idle daughters at home. One of them will come to you and chase the Devil off by praying at her bedside. I have raised them well. Even though they are ladies, they know all kinds of work. They will help around the house while your wife is confined to her childbed. You only have to promise me that you'll make me the godmother of the little one."

The poor man's heart almost burst out of his chest with joy because he knew his wife was already pregnant again. He went home and told her about the conversation and how kind the Captain's wife had been to them. At first, she did not even want to believe it, but he swore up and down that it was all true. She found out soon enough when the guards brought their cows back home. The men didn't only hand back the livestock, but they also noted how dilapidated the cottage was. They went straight to the Captain's wife and reported that the poor couple indeed had nothing and no one to their name, even with the stork already nesting on their roof.

"Well then, Marika, we can't wait any longer," the lady told her youngest daughter. "Pack your things, and I will prepare a basket that you can take with you. Tell the driver to bring the carriage around."

Marika got ready quickly. The only things she packed were a drywood (a kind of fiddle) and a small box. She held the instrument under her chin, and as she drew a small whip across it, it played wonderful melodies. Marika could play it so exquisitely that crying babies would begin to laugh, and people who laughed all their life would weep. In the box, there was a beautiful book full of stories.

The moment the carriage stopped in front of the poor man's house, Marika bolted inside, hugged the wife, and said to her, "Dear Auntie, do not worry. I will be here until the little Gyurka, or little Marika arrives. I will play this drywood so beautifully, you will not even feel the pain. And if you are about to fall asleep, I have this book. It has such wonderful stories in it, they will brighten your heart. I will not let you or the baby slip away. I promise."

The poor woman felt relief wash over her. She wouldn't be alone anymore when her time came. The Devil wouldn't take the baby as soon as it arrived from the long journey.

Marika barely sat down when the wife cried out, "Oh! Oh! The Devil is coming! It is right there by the window!"

Marika was not alarmed. She did not look for the imaginary Devil. Instead, she ran outside to the poor man and told him to go get the midwife because, if his wife was seeing the Devil, the little one must be on his way. And lo and behold, the poor man *did* run like the Devil was chasing him.

The midwife didn't live far, and they returned soon enough. They sent the little girl outside. She barely waited a few minutes when she saw the poor man step out, his face a mix of joy and worry. Marika ran to him and hugged him, kissing him on the cheek.

"Do not worry, dear Uncle. I will be here every single day for a week while you work. My mother will send for me in the evenings, and if, God forbid, there is any trouble, she will send my eldest sister, too. I will read and play music to help the Lady and the little boy sleep. It is a boy, isn't it?"

"A boy. It is a boy, and what a boy! He bounces in the midwife's hands."

They went in. The poor woman was tired, but she was not afraid of the Devil anymore. She knew that if it was needed, the darling little girl would protect her baby with tooth and nail. The moment Marika walked in, the poor woman couldn't thank her enough. Marika wiped her forehead with a handkerchief and said, "Dear Lady, save your strength. It is the duty of all people to help others. That is how my mother taught me. That is how my teacher taught me. That is what I believe."

The house was filled with joy. The poor man went to work, the poor woman slept, and Marika guarded her sleep and the child. For a week, the carriage brought Marika at dawn every morning. A lady like Marika did not need to wake with the sun, but she did anyway to help the poor couple. She played music, read stories from the book, and made sure the little family was well cared for.

Time went by. Little Gyuri could now walk, even run, and he was visited almost every day by the Captain's daughters. They loved him like a little brother. He had everything he could wish for.

When he was about two years old, the Captain's wife told her second daughter, "Zsuzsika, you should go to the poor man's house today. They are expecting the stork again, and the wife might be afraid of the Devil. Be smart, my dear, and brave. Don't disappoint me."

The little lady packed her things, and the carriage took her to the cottage. By the time she got there, the poor woman was in bed, shivering with terror. She didn't even need to say anything; Zsuzsika was already running for the husband to tell him to fetch the midwife right away. The midwife soon came. By that time, the poor woman was in so much pain that it was a pity to see. The poor man took Zsuzsika outside, and there she consoled him. She pulled out a strange little drum, and beating on it, she sang so sweetly that the poor man forgot about his fears and worries.

Suddenly, the midwife called out, "Come on in, good man, I have your daughter! She is so lively I can barely hold her. She'll sleep so well, the milk will envy her. But come quickly, your wife is falling asleep. You can't let her or she will never wake up."

Before the poor man could move, Zsuzsika was already inside. She pulled a chair to the bedside and talked to the poor woman.

"Auntie, look! What a blessing she is. Look! They are putting her in the cradle now. Look at her! In a week or two, you will be holding her in your arms with joy. She is such a beauty! I have never seen a child this beautiful in all my life!"

She chatted and chatted, keeping the wife awake. Finally, they handed the baby to the poor woman. Indeed, the baby was so beautiful that she could have been a fairy. The poor woman was radiant with joy. She asked Zsuzsika to stay and promised to name the baby girl after her, if their mother allowed it.

Zsuzsika visited the house every day for a week, looking after her little namesake and bringing gifts for the family. The poor woman was soon out of childbed, and the little girl was growing more beautiful every day. Marika and Zsuzsika played with her, dressed her like a doll, and did not allow her mother to go out for any work. They brought work to the house instead, a little sewing and embroidery. The Captains' daughters paid the poor woman well for it so that she couldn't say she lived on charity alone.

When it rains, it pours – and blessings did pour onto the house. Soon the wife was carrying a third child. When her time came, the eldest daughter of the Captain went to visit. She was a very kind girl, but a little chatty. When the wife began to cry and scream that the Devil was coming to take all her children, little lady Ágneske calmed her so nicely, holding her hand, that tears welled up in the wife's eyes. She asked Ágneske how it could be that wealthy ladies, like her and her sisters, could be so compassionate to poor people like this family.

"Dear Auntie, our mother taught us that there is no difference between people, except between the kind and the unkind. We saw that you and Uncle were kind, and therefore we needed to help you. Believe me, Auntie, it brought us as much joy to be here as it did to you. I am happy that we could be godmothers to these beautiful children. May I be godmother to the one coming now? I have already put away some silver coins in case it is a boy. If it is a girl, I will give her my favorite doll."

Ágneske barely finished the sentence when the poor woman began screaming in pain. Ágneske ran to the poor man, telling him to fetch the midwife quick for she had been chatting too long, and time was of the essence. As luck would have it, the midwife was already on her way. She had seen the Captain's carriage pulling up to the cottage and, being a wise woman, she had learned by now what that meant.

Things happened quickly from there. Ágneske and the poor man barely had time to step outside when the midwife was already calling for them to bring warm water because the baby was born sick. Ágneske worked like a whirlwind, lighting a fire, heating the water, warming a shawl to bundle the baby. But, in the end, the most important thing was love. Her loving care healed the baby in just a few hours, and it began wailing stronger than a month-old child. The Mother and Ágneske laughed with relief at the sound. The little lady brought her favorite doll the very next day. Her mother said it was too early to give a doll to a newborn, but she brought it anyway so that Lidike could play (that was how they named the baby girl).

The three ladies and the three children lived like siblings. They visited each other every day. The Captain gave a good job to the poor man, and the poor woman was hired as head cook in his house. The three ladies grew up as kind as they were beautiful, and famous in all the land for both. The poor man and his wife prayed every day to God to reward the ladies for their kindness. And He did – all three of them married gentle, loving husbands, just the kind they deserved. They all named the two little girls as their bridesmaids, and Gyurika as their best man. They all got married on the same day in a wedding the splendor of which no one had ever seen before. Everyone who looked at the brides and the three children thought that they were truly siblings. It is no wonder they did, for the Captain's wife dressed the little girls like her own daughters, and dressed the boy as if he had been her son.

It was a beautiful wedding. The three children sat so happily at the head table as if it had been their own wedding feast. I have no doubt that whenever it came to that, their weddings were just as joyful, too.

It is rare as a white raven for one family to not look down on another. But this story is true. And also beautiful.

**Comments**

It is rare to see childbirth portrayed in such a realistic way in a tale. This story, told by a woman and collected by a woman, revolves around a woman's fear of giving birth and losing a child – a fear that was both constantly present and well-founded before modern medicine. It contains endearing details that, despite the lack of talking animals or meddling fairies, make it a magical tale. It contains a whole cast of likable female characters, from the Captain's competent wife, through the chatty eldest daughter, all the way to the wise old midwife. These fine women don't only support each other, but also take time to extend their love and care to the slightly terrified father-to-be.

This time, unlike in the previous folktale, all three daughters get their turn to shine, and with their own names as well, which makes telling a story with this many female characters significantly less confusing. Marika (Mary), Zsuzsika (Susan), and Ágneske (Agnes) take turns caring for Gyurika (George), Zsuzsika the Younger, and Lidike (Lydia or Ildikó). All their names are diminutive nicknames commonly used in Hungarian. I disentangled the tale a little. In the original text, names were sometimes confused and the sequence of events occasionally out of order, especially in the end where the triple wedding became mixed up with hopes of another, future one.

The language of this tale is particularly colorful, and I tried to translate it as close to the original as possible. There are multiple references to the stork that, much like in other Western traditions, is responsible for bringing newborn babies. There are also phrases like "she will sleep so well the milk will envy her" (in Hungarian, curds are called *aludttej*, "sleeping milk"), and "she was lively like a *csík*" (*csík* being a type of fish, a weather loach, that tends to wiggle a lot) – I translated this latter one as "bouncing." I left Anna's own description of the "drywood" in the text. A drywood is a fiddle-like instrument, but apparently even her contemporary audiences were not sure of the meaning of the word anymore because she had to explain it.

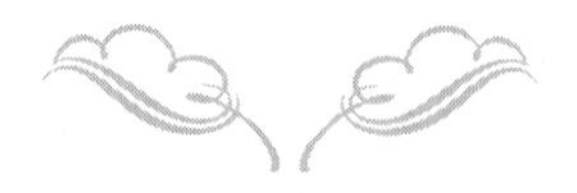

# The Joy of the Princess

I have told you tales about kings, knights, dwarves, and more. Now I want to tell you one about a princess.

Once upon a time, up in the mountains, there was a beautiful castle. In the castle lived a prince. He owned everything as far as the eye could see and even beyond that for two days' distance. He had good land that yielded great wine, which was famous near and far. The house was always filled with music and merriment. The Prince's wife was a sickly, skinny woman who did not care much for parties, but his daughter made up for her mother's lack of interest with a passionate love for entertainment and all things beautiful.

One day, word came that the Turkish Emperor was going to visit them and purchase some wine. The Prince only half believed the news, at first, because he had heard that Turkish people only drank wine for blessings and, since they did not bless very often, they also didn't drink. But the news was soon confirmed, and the Prince began to prepare for the illustrious guest. Oxen and sheep were fattened and butchered, cooks were hired, and everyone waited for the Emperor's arrival with excitement. Everyone, that is, except for the Prince's wife, who fell so ill that she was not likely to live to see the visit. All kinds of doctors and wise women were called immediately to make her better. The Prince was worried that he might lose his beloved wife and that they would have to greet their great guest in mourning.

The wife was beginning to heal just when the Emperor arrived. And what a man he was! The moment the Princess laid eyes on him, she fell deeply in love. Not with the Emperor – but with the gorgeous, embroidered kaftan he was wearing! She pictured in her mind what an incredible Sunday dress she could make from that garment. Such a piece of finery would turn all heads and make all women shiver with envy. She immediately went to her father and began coaxing him into asking for the kaftan as the price for the wine. For you see, if she could not wear it on Pentecost Day, she insisted, she would surely die.

"Even if it takes all the wine in my cellars, you will have it, my darling flower," the Prince, who had been thoroughly wrapped around his daughter's dainty little finger, promised immediately. The promise was overheard by a clever servant and soon reached the ears of the Turkish Emperor. Now the Emperor was also clever and, on top of that, was in love with the Princess from the moment they had met.

The feast began along with the negotiations over the price of the wine. The Prince told his guest that he was willing to offer as much wine as he wanted if the Emperor gave his kaftan in return as a keepsake for the Prince's daughter. The Emperor pretended to be upset. Did the Prince imagine him going home naked?! And to hand over a garment that had been handed down from one emperor to the next for generations?! It took more negotiation, and more wine, for the Emperor to begin warming up to the idea... or so it appeared. In the end, the Emperor agreed, but only on the condition that he could help the Princess try on the kaftan. The Prince saw nothing wrong with that.

"Be as you wish, Your Majesty."

The Princess and the Emperor were sent to another room to wiggle in and out of clothing with no witnesses around. But as soon as they closed the door and began to undress, another one opened. In wandered the Prince's wife, just out of her sickbed, staring with wide-eyed shock at her daughter and the Emperor. The girl, joyful that her mother was up and about, hugged and kissed her and shared the exciting news that the Emperor was going to give her his gorgeous kaftan for the wine. The Prince's wife was not very impressed with the exchange, but she was happy for her daughter's excitement. She asked to see how the kaftan would look on her beautiful daughter.

The Emperor took off the kaftan. Under it, he was wearing a simple white shirt, one that went all the way to his ankles. He was far from naked, but the Princess still blushed at the sight. The Emperor helped the Princess into the kaftan and, since he already had his arms around her, he also embraced her. She did not mind at all. Then he kissed her, and she did not mind that either. She kissed him right back. The mother almost fainted.

Since the kaftan fitting seemed to be taking quite a long time, the Prince walked in to see how it was progressing. He saw his daughter with the Emperor. Then he saw his wife, standing upright, but about to fall again. So, he gave a chuckle, caught his wife in his arms and kissed her. The Princess looked at her parents and laughed, "I can see my father and mother are just as happy for the kaftan as I am!"

The Emperor asked for the Princess's hand in marriage right then and there. It was not a simple decision. The Prince knew that Turkish men had twenty or even more wives, so he asked for time to consider his daughter's best interest. He would have gladly given all his wine for his daughter's happiness, but would never give his daughter in marriage for even a hundred kaftans. She was his only child, after all. However, the issue was soon resolved when the Emperor offered to stay and live as the dutiful son of the Prince, if only he be allowed to marry the Princess. Everyone rejoiced. The Princess kissed her father, her mother, and the Emperor. Then she danced around the castle in her new kaftan. She was a vision like no other, so beautiful it brought tears to people's eyes.

This is how the Princess found happiness. The Emperor was a good man and made a husband like no other. They had a great wedding with much wine. Even those who didn't drink the wine got drunk on pure joy.

May all of those who look for a new kaftan find such happiness in the end.

## Comments

It is endearing to find a tale like this, given the tumultuous history of Eastern Europe with the Ottoman Empire. The Turks often appear as villains or even monsters in Hungarian tales. The history of the Turkish wars permeates our classic literature, art, and grade school textbooks. One would be hard-pressed to find a Hungarian folktale with a friendly Turkish character in it – let alone a love interest. And yet, here we have a princess that does not only fall in love with an emperor, but she also falls in love with the (typically Eastern) garment he wears.

While the historical accuracy of Pályuk's story is questionable, I left the tale as I found it. Her hints at the "Emperor" (not sultan) breaking Islam's ban on consuming alcohol, the musings about the possibility of twenty-plus wives, and the implication that the Emperor would leave his country to its fate all belong to the story. These things make the story more carelessly cheerful and fairy tale-like. Once again, I had to decide about translating *herceg*. For the sake of saying 'princess' instead of 'duke's daughter' every single time, I decided on "prince" for this story.

*"It was such a wedding,"* notes Anna after the end of this story, *"That Uncle Laci would still be drunk today if he was still alive."* It is always good of the storyteller to get her audience involved – even if they are dead.

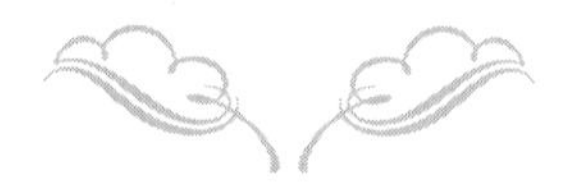

# The Woodcutter's Luck

Once upon a time, there was a vast oak forest. In the middle of the forest, there was a neat little castle. No one knew who lived there, and everyone was afraid to find out because eerie rumors surrounded the place. Rumors of whispers of the cursed soul of a headless man that walked around at night; the sound of weeping heard outside the castle walls before dawn; and a mysterious figure visiting every month during the new moon. This is what was said, and this was what people believed. Everyone was terrified to go anywhere near the castle, and whoever lived there did not seem to mind being left alone.

One night, a terrible storm blew through the land. It uprooted several old oak trees around the castle. The fallen trees blocked the gates so no one could go in or out. Not that many people ever tried to go in unless they had serious business that could not be avoided, but for those who lived inside, being trapped in the castle would have meant certain death. Soon word came from the mysterious owners of the castle that whoever cleared away the trees could keep all the wood and would also get paid. Even with the promise of such a rich reward, everyone was too afraid to go–except for one poor woodcutter. He had three sons and two daughters, all of them hard-working children, and they went together to clear the fallen trees.

As they worked, they kept glancing nervously towards the castle. They did not see a single soul trying to go in or come out all day. No one even *looked* outside to see how things were progressing. As evening fell, the children went to sleep, one by one, until only the woodcutter remained awake to keep watch. It was almost dark when he heard hooves. Shortly after, the silhouette of a rider appeared on the road. He clapped in excitement when he saw that the gates had been freed from the rubble. He knocked, the gates opened, and he disappeared inside. In a few moments, music started drifting out from the castle; music so beautiful that the woodcutter's heart twisted with awe. When midnight passed, the music stopped, and the gates opened again. The mysterious man rode away without glancing back. The moment he left, silence turned to weeping, so heartbreakingly sad that it could have softened the rocks on the mountain. The woodcutter's kind heart ached for whoever had such sorrow in their life, but there was nothing he could do.

In the morning, the family continued working hard. Together, they managed to clear all the trees away in three days' time. The woodcutter witnessed the same thing every night. The last night, his youngest son also woke up and heard it all. In the morning, he began to tell his siblings when his father snapped at him, telling him to keep his mouth shut and his hands busy. But curiosity had already nested in the boy's heart, and he was determined to uncover the castle's secret.

Once they had all the wood chopped, it was time to load it on a cart and take it back to the village. They had enough to fill the yard of a wealthy man, and they had to make several trips to transport it all. When the woodcutter and his children were loading the last cartful, they were stopped by a gamekeeper who asked what they had seen. The woodcutter considered the question for a moment and then answered.

"Whatever I heard and saw, I will not tell anyone. I don't know who lives here or who comes here, and I don't know what happens inside the walls. I have no stories to tell."

"If you truly can keep a secret like that, then take this pouch of gold. As long as your silence lasts, you will receive one just like it every year."

The woodcutter liked this deal. Now he had wood to sell and money to spend. He built a nice large house, and he married his daughters to good men from the best families in the village. His elder sons married well, too, but the youngest refused to choose a bride. In secret, he sneaked to the forest occasionally to watch the castle, but he always fell asleep, so he never saw the rider or heard the weeping again… until one evening, when he was stung by a large fly on his cheek. The pain kept him awake. This time he saw the handsome rider knock on the gate and be let in. He heard the cheerful music, and he also heard the weeping after the rider left. *What does this all mean?* The boy wondered and resolved to find out more the following night.

The next evening, he found a hiding place closer to the gates. When the rider arrived, he crouched under the horse's belly and, as the gates were opened, he slipped inside, too.

In the middle of the courtyard, he saw a table set for a feast. Next to the table, hung between two oak trees, there was a hammock. In the swinging bed, reclined a beautiful girl. She didn't have legs. She lay on silken pillows, motionless, until the rider walked up to her. Only then did she sit up, with light in her eyes, and with such excitement, she almost overturned the hammock. The rider took out a little box and, from the box, a flute. He played beautiful music until the girl fell asleep. Then he ate a little from the table, and an old servant opened the gates to let him out. Soon after he left, the girl woke up, saw that she was alone, and began to weep. She wept until morning.

The boy did not know who these people were or why they were acting so strangely, but he wanted to find out more. So, he stayed. To his misfortune, in the morning light, the old servant found him and chased him until the boy fell into a deep pit. As he looked around, he realized he was not alone in there. He was sharing his captivity with the Father of all Devils. *This is not good*, he thought. *I need to do something about this.*

The Devil spoke first.

"Listen, boy, I am just as trapped here as you are. But I intend to leave soon and, if you help, I will take you with me."

The boy would have done anything to escape the pit, so he agreed.

"All I need for us to escape is your hair," the Devil said.

The boy, not thinking twice about it, allowed him to cut his hair. The Devil pulled out shearing scissors and cut it down to the skin. He occasionally nicked the skin, too, but the boy was too scared to wince or complain. By the morning light, the Devil braided the hair into a long piece of rope.

"Now, jump and throw this rope up to that tree outside the pit."

But no matter how many times the boy jumped, he could not throw the rope far enough. So, the Devil did. He climbed out first. The moment he was out, he pulled up the rope, threw it away, and disappeared with a mocking laugh.

Whether the boy is still there in the pit or not, I can't tell you.

The woodcutter waited for his son to come home, but he never did. After a while, he began to suspect that the boy must have gone back to the castle.

He told his wife, "I will go and see if I can find our son. But if I don't return, don't try to follow me."

The wife cried and didn't want to let him go, but he had made up his mind.

The woodcutter hid close to the castle gates, waiting for someone to appear. When someone did, it was not a person he had wished to see. The Father of Devils walked up to him with a smirk on his face.

"Your son is inside," he said. "We were in there together, but he fell asleep, didn't hear the rooster crow, and when the gates opened and closed, he was trapped inside. They must have kept him as a servant."

The woodcutter thought that serving in the castle was not too bad a job. But the Devil, who was intent on destroying the woodcutter as he had destroyed his son, pulled out a fist-sized rock from his satchel.

"The only way you will *ever* see your son again is if you wait for the rider, and then throw this rock at him."

But the woodcutter was not about to listen to the Devil. He took the rock, weighed it in his palm for a moment, and threw it so far away no one ever saw it land. The Devil, more scared of an honest man than anything else in the world, fled the scene in a puff of smoke.

No sooner did the Devil disappear that the gates opened, and out came the old servant.

"You have honor and a good heart. I saw what happened. For what you have done, these gates will always be open to you and your family. I built this castle for my daughter, who was born without legs and didn't want to live among people who would mock her. But you are kind, and so is your family. Come live with us. My son is the greatest lord in all the land, he owns the forest, the mountain, and everything you see. He sent you all that money, and he will give you more if you serve us well. A musician comes here every night. He is in love with my daughter, but they cannot be together, for his father is the Father of all Devils. He wants to destroy their love by any means, and whenever the boy is not here to play music, my daughter weeps and weeps. Now you know all our secrets. You can decide how much of it you want to tell your family. The only thing I ask is that you don't ask any questions, and don't tell anyone else about what you see inside these walls."

The woodcutter told his wife that he was going to work in the castle. It was only fair, he argued, after they received all that money year after year.

"If you go, I go, too," said his wife.

So, they walked to the castle together and, for the first time, they found the gates wide open. Inside, there was the hammock between the trees and the legless girl in it. The woodcutter's wife began to cry from pity that such a beautiful girl would be locked up in such a lonely place. The girl was startled at first to see so many strangers, but her father told her not to worry as they were good people.

The woodcutter's wife pulled up a chair and told the girl about her own daughters to cheer the girl. She even offered to send her daughters to keep the girl company. However, they could only come in the afternoon after they were done with housework since they all had their own households now. The girl asked her to send a daughter the very next day, and so she did, sending her youngest daughter.

The girl in the castle was excited to make such a pretty friend almost her age. They talked all day about the girl's husband, and her baby who could not walk yet, but was very lively. The girl asked to see the baby, and the next time the woodcutter's daughter visited, she brought her son along. The legless girl played cheerfully all day with the child, gave him gifts, and called him her darling flower. The boy tumbled around on her pillows and swung in the hammock squealing with joy. He barely wanted to leave in the evening. So, the girl asked the mother to leave the boy with her. When the boy didn't want to go home the next day either or the day after, the young woman and her husband had to move into the castle. The old servant made the couple his heirs of the castle, grateful that they loved his daughter like family.

The musician, once he learned that his devil father was not lurking around the castle anymore, returned, and was greeted with laughter and open gates. The legless girl was radiant with joy when she saw him, and from that moment on, there was music within the walls day and night—and no weeping at all.

## Comments

Several of Anna's tales involve men and women, princes and princesses, who are missing limbs (see *The Daughter of the Táltos King* in the last chapter). In one story, not included in this book, even her dragon-killing hero only has one hand. I have always wondered where that image came from or whether she had someone in her own life who had this kind of a disability. She always talks about these characters with empathy and makes sure that they end up happy. In this story, the fears, curiosity, and kindness of everyday people meet a world that is infused with just a hint of magic and surrounded by rumors. In the end, it is the kindness that opens the gates of a locked, lonely home.

I changed a few small things in my telling of this tale. Originally, when the woodcutter tells his son to keep quiet about the castle, he slaps him hard. In addition, when the wife first sees the legless girl, she cries out of pity that "such a beautiful girl could be a cripple." Since I don't use these elements when I tell this story, I did not include them in the text here, either. I also took out the part where, by the end of the story, the woodcutter had *three* daughters instead of two, and he took one of them along on their first visit. Since she didn't do anything until the next day, I decided to leave her out. Besides, the hesitant wife meeting the legless girl one on one gave the scene a more intimate feel.

*Muzsika* ("music") is a word that can be used for multiple instruments from a fiddle to a type of ocarina. I translated it as a "flute" for clarity's sake and because it seemed like a softer choice for a lullaby than a fiddle. "Father of All Devils" is my translation for Öregördög, the Old Devil. The musician's return at the end of the story is my addition. Anna probably forgot about it once she got immersed in describing the fortunes of the woodcutter's family. I could not resist bringing him back, especially since his father, the Öregördög, had been chased away. I was tempted to bring the woodcutter's curious son back as well and, if you wish, you most certainly may. Furicz János had a very similar story in his repertoire. In that one, the castle's mysterious lady was the Daughter of the Wind King. She ended up marrying the curious boy who first stole inside the walls.

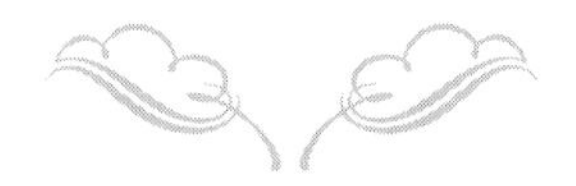

# The Devil's Godfather

Once upon a time, close to the edge of the world, there was a bottomless well. In that well (or so they say), there lived an old dragon with his mother. No one has seen them, mind you, not even I. I only heard it from my mother in the spinning house when she was in a good mood, and I will tell it to you as she told it to me.

Close to the well, there was a village and a city. One time, disaster swept across the land for two years, and there was not a single drop of rain. All the rivers went dry, and so did all the wells. Livestock was dying of thirst, for they don't last as long without water as people do. Even people were beginning to drop, one after another. They organized a procession to the big well to pray or conjure up some water, but it was all in vain. It was then that the old women of the village suggested that they should ask the Devil for help since God was obviously not listening, despite the prayers and the fasts. Maybe the Devil would be more willing? But where could they find him? Everyone was asking the same question, and no one could answer it. Finally, they all went to the city to ask a very old lawyer where the Devil lived.

"Sure, I can tell you. I have worked with him all my life," the lawyer said. "Just be careful not to regret it. You have chosen a good time to seek him out. He is preparing for a baptism and, if he is in a good mood, he might just help you."

With that, the old lawyer gave the place at such and such a crossroads, on such and such a day, at such and such an hour where they could find the Devil. But he also told them to pray on it, and pray on it hard before they resolved to call on him.

The village decided to send the priest to talk with the Devil. The priest was not thrilled about the idea, but there was no excuse. He was simply the most qualified person for the job. He went to the crossroads on a Sunday at midnight with his heart in his throat, muttering prayers. When the Devil called out to him, he almost jumped out of his skin with fright.

"Lucky you have come, Father, because my wife just gave birth to our ninety-seventh boy, and we have run out of relatives to be godparents!"

Whether he wanted it or not, the priest had to accept becoming the godfather of the newborn baby devil. However, the priest had his wits about him, and he complied on one condition: the Devil would help them end the draught and send the village some much-needed water.

"Very well," the Devil agreed. "By the time you return home, there will be enough water for everyone. But don't forget to show up for the baptism, or I will have to come and fetch you."

And so, it was. The villagers didn't know (or didn't want to know) where the water in their wells came from. They were just happy to have it. But trouble soon followed, for the city still had no water. People came down from the city to the village at night and took all the water they could find. The next day the village judge ordered guards to find out who was stealing the water. Every household sent a man to join the guard. As night fell, the guardsmen all saw the same thing. People pouring out of the city, down to the wells, drawing, and carrying all the water back home. The villagers attacked them to scare them away. Threats soon became a brawl, and the brawl turned into a miniature battlefield.

Finally, some of the people from the city noticed that water was flowing to the village from the direction of the great old well. They thought that if the old well could give water to the village, maybe it could supply the city, too. Since they were tired of being beaten by the villagers, they went to see about the well.

On the edge of the well, sat the Devil's wife with a beautiful bouncing baby in her arms. When the city's judge asked her if they could have water, she shrugged.

"I know nothing about that. I am waiting here because it is time for my son's baptism and my husband has gone to fetch the godfather. If you wish to talk to him, you can wait with me."

So, they waited for two whole days. The city people were bored, and they had to send someone to the city for food. Eventually, most people dispersed, leaving only the city judge to represent their claims. Neither the Devil nor the godfather appeared until the third evening. You see, the Devil had a bit of a hard time convincing the priest to come along. When they finally arrived, the Devil was carrying the priest on his back like a sack of flour - a sight which alarmed the city judge.

"What are you doing here?" the Devil asked as he stopped and set the priest on his feet.

"I-I-I... I came here to wish you all the best for the baptism!"

"You are a good man," said the Devil. "You know what? I know the city has no water, so I will send some for you, too, on one condition. You have to promise that you won't collect taxes this year."

The judge agreed immediately. No one could have paid anyway having no crops and no cattle. He also thought that, whenever people got their wealth back, he could always declare some extra taxes and make up for the difference. So, he gave his word.

"Let us put it into writing," the Devil insisted. "I have been cheated by many people in my life, and I don't want to be cheated again."

So, they called the old lawyer and drew up an agreement. The judge went home to share the happy news with the city.

Once they were alone, the Devil told the priest, "Father, I want my son to be named Simon."

"Very well, he'll be named Simon," agreed the priest. The priest would have agreed to any name if the whole ordeal concluded quickly. But the Devil's wife resisted; she wanted to name her son Mihály.

"We can name him Mihály," the priest agreed to that, too. But in the end, the child was named neither Simon nor Mihály because the baby spoke and said, "Dear Mother, dear Father, my name is Pluto and nothing else!"

"If you are Pluto, you will be Pluto if you behave yourself," the Devil told his youngest son with a pat on his head. "And we will give you, name and all, to your godfather to raise."

*What will I do with this boy?* The priest thought, alarmed by the prospect. *I can't take him home with me or the village will start rumors that I stole a child from a Gypsy woman or got it some other sordid way! What shall I do?!*

"Don't worry about me, godfather, I can make myself so small I will fit in your pocket! No one will notice me," said the devil boy. Then he immediately shrunk to the size of a large apple and hopped into the priest's pocket. He wiggled occasionally, so the priest had to pat his pocket to keep him calm.

As soon as the priest returned to the village, he saw that something was wrong. People were crying and wailing everywhere. The priest stopped a man on the street and asked him what had happened.

"Tragedy, father! Tragedy! All the children in the village have suddenly shrunk to the size of an apple! They are lively as ever. They are alive, but cursed! We were about to look for you and ask you to celebrate mass to remove the curse."

The priest knew a mass would not help. They had water now, but trouble came with it in the form of a tiny devil boy. He didn't say anything to the man. Instead, he walked into the church and pulled his godson out of his pocket.

"Listen, Pluto, this will not do at all. If every child is like you, then the village will be in great trouble. We are already struggling with how little water we have. The good people of my flock do not need any more things to worry about."

"Oh Godfather, I know how things could be better, but a lot of bravery is needed for that."

"Tell me, dear godson."

"It is all the old well's fault," the little devil explained. "You know, the one at the edge of the village. The old dragon lives in there with his mother. The woman is at least a thousand years old, and the dragon is not much younger. They are old, but they are strong. They have been hoarding the water for themselves. My father serves them, but he can only coax out the water little by little. If someone could kill the dragons, there would be enough water for everyone. But who could do such a thing?"

"Indeed, who?" wondered the priest. He did not have to wonder for long because soon the door of the church banged open and in rolled a very handsome little boy! He was also the size of an apple, a small one at that, but he was dragging a sword behind him. A sword so long it almost reached from one end of the church to the other.

"Well then, Father, I will kill the dragon and its mother today! If you don't mind."

The priest did not mind at all, except he was afraid the dragons would laugh at the boy and swallow him whole.

"Who are you, my son?" he asked, squinting at the tiny figure.

"I am a godson of yours, the son of the bell-ringer of your church! Don't you recognize me?"

"Now I do! Look, Pluto, here is another godson of mine. He is willing to kill the dragons. What say you?"

"I will go and help him by drinking the water that bursts from the well. Don't worry, godfather. Once the dragons are dead, there will be rain and all the wells will fill up again."

The priest nodded to Pluto, and at that moment the devil boy grew as tall as the church tower. But not just him; the bell ringer's son and all the other children in the village sprang up as well! The whole place looked like a forest walking around, a forest of flailing legs and arms. Pluto and his new brother, ready for their quest, walked from the village together. The rest of the children stayed, laughing happily as they chased terrified cows or crying as they got their fingers stuck in chimneys.

The priest watched the scene in shock and thought... *What shall I do?! Will the children ever shrink back to their normal size? Are we to live in a village full of giant children from now on? I wish Pluto's father were here, he'd know what to do.* As soon as he thought that, the Devil appeared in a puff of sulfur from behind one of the painted saints.

"I can see you care for my boy, and you want him to be a good man, Father. Tell me, what's wrong? Why do you need my help?"

"There is much trouble, and only you can help," the priest said. As the Devil stepped closer, the priest suddenly felt uneasy. He began to back away and reached for the incense burner to smoke him out. Just then, the Devil caught him and shook him.

"What is it?!"

"I-I-I only want the dragons dead so we can have water! Don't hurt me!"

"That is all? My son can do that for you. But if he can't, I'll take you with me."

While the priest wondered, terrified, whether he would go to Hell or not, his godson was already at work. The boy had grown to love his godfather, even more than his own father, and he was determined to defeat the dragons. It was a terrible fight. When the dragons saw that they had worthy opponents, they began spewing water from the well. There was so much water that it would have flooded the entire world had Pluto not gulped it down. He drank, and he drank, and he drank. While he was drinking, his sworn brother chopped off the dragons' heads, one after another. Only when the last head rolled to the ground, did the flood stop. Pluto and his brother dragged the bodies out of the well and burned them. They found a dragon egg at the bottom, Pluto crushed it under his foot, and that was the end of dragonkind in this world. The wind picked up pieces of the rough skin of the dragon's mother. The pieces swirled in the air, fell to the ground, and hopped away: this is how the first toads were born.

As the flames on the pyre sprang up, lightning flashed across the sky and clouds gathered with thunder.

Some children jumped and squealed, but most people laughed and yelled, "Rain! Rain! The rain is coming! There will be rain, there will be snow, there will be a harvest, and everything will be well again!"

They were so busy celebrating that they didn't even notice when the bell ringer's son collapsed to the ground. He had been struck with the evil eye by one of the dragons and died from it.

Pluto and his godfather told the villagers all that happened. They explained the apple-sized children, the invasion of giants, the lack of water, and the death of the dragons. The bell ringer's son received a hero's funeral, and his memory lived on for generations. The priest kept his sword safe in the church as a memento of all that had transpired. The villagers eventually also learned that there had been not one, but two, godsons, and the one that survived was the child of the Devil. But knowing the whole tale by now, they didn't mind at all.

This is how the story ends. Pluto still lives with the priest, in his pocket, small as an apple. Sometimes he wiggles, and the priest pats his pocket to calm him down. He made a good godfather. If you ever need one, make sure to look him up.

**Comments**

In the Hungarian oral tradition, the Devil is not always the personification of all evil, and neither is it one single character. There are multiple devils such as little devils (*kisördög*) and old devils (öreg ördög); they have mothers, wives, children, and apparently even godfathers. In fact, young devils are often rather mischievous and occasionally helpful to heroes on their journey. In a Bukovinian *Székely* folktale (adapted into a beautiful cartoon), Pinkó, the son of the Devil, similarly helps a poor man accomplish impossible tasks. In one folktale from Ung County, the hero of the story is the Devil's son, who rescues a princess from the Glass Mountain and marries her in the end. In another one, collected by Berze Nagy János, a devil child exiled from Hell for being too soft-hearted helps a similarly exiled mortal boy save a kingdom. Devils are usually portrayed as dark-skinned (which is why the priest worries someone will mistake his godson for a stolen Roma child), but in the original text of this tale, the Devil's wife is also described as "dark-skinned, yet beautiful." Given that I tell to contemporary audiences, I don't include these details any-more, but they are a part of the older tradition.

By agreeing to be the godfather of this child, the priest becomes attached to the Devil. They call each other *koma*, which is a term used for non-blood related bonds between people, most often through serving as godparents in baptism (similar to the Spanish *compadre*). Even more importantly, the priest proves to be a good father figure for Pluto and thus helps save the village and the city from the draught. Anna notes that even the Devil will not harm a priest, ever since one of them became a *koma* to him.

The real villain of the story is the dragon who lives with his mother in the well. A monster keeping the life-preserving water supply from the people is a very common motif all around the world, most generally recognized in the West as the legend of Saint George. While the Devil, as the dragon's servant, clearly has some say in the water distribution, dragonkind must be killed in the end for the good of humanity. It is this element of the tale – the dragon in the well – that hints that this story might have been longer and more detailed once upon a time. In Anna's telling, the entire fight was glossed over; we only learned about it after the fact. I added a more elaborate description and restored the fight scene itself.

My favorite moment in this story is the Devil's request to put an agreement in writing. "Cheating the Devil" tales are extremely popular in Hungary, so much so that they have their own *volume* in the Hungar-ian Folktale Index. No wonder the Devil wants some insurance signed and witnessed!

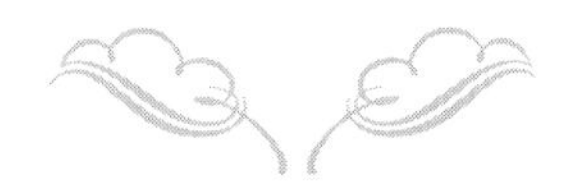

# The Little Swineherd

Once upon a time, across the Óperenciás Sea and even beyond that by a flea's jump, there lived an old woman. She had three sons; all of them good, all of them smart, and all of them afraid of their mother—for sometimes she beat them quite badly. If they did not bring wood from the forest, forgot their chores, or broke something around the house, she would strike them. She was quite a strong woman, too. She did the laundry for the priest, for the inn, and other places that needed work. She also washed the dead and, in exchange, received all their clothes, which is how she dressed her sons. They were dressed in all kinds of mismatched clothing, winter clothes in the summer, summer clothes in the winter, but at least they got them for free. It was a big village, and people died all the time.

One day, the woman told her sons, "Boys, I have worked enough; I am tired, and all the rubbing is eating away at my hands. You are all grown men now. It is only fair that you should look for work and take care of me for a change."

The three boys were at a loss; none of them had ever learned a profession. But since they all loved their mother, they decided to find work so that they could take care of her. The eldest went to the blacksmith.

"Master Blacksmith, would you take me on as an apprentice?"

"You have come at the right time, son. There is much work to do. The King ordered 200 meters of wire fence so tightly woven that not even a mosquito can pass through it. I need more hands to make it."

So, the boy stayed. When he got hungry from all the work, he sat down by the river and pulled out the ash cake his mother had baked for the road. As he sat there eating, an ant appeared and asked him for a morsel. The boy chased it away saying he barely had enough food for himself. The ant left without saying another word.

The boy worked hard for the rest of the day without food or drink. The master had water inside the house, but he was angry at his new apprentice for accidentally hitting his hand with the hammer sometimes, so he did not give him any. The boy hoped he would get dinner for his work, but instead he was sent to bed hungry. As he lay down on his cot, he noticed a roasted goose leg on the ground covered in ants. He was so hungry, so he decided to eat it despite the ants. But as he grabbed it, the ants swarmed over his hand and bit him in a million places.

The ants said, "You did not give us even a morsel of your ash cake. Why should we give you our food? Leave us!"

The boy fell asleep hungry. In his dream, he saw a royal city. In the royal city was a splendid castle. In the castle, there was an old king desperately looking for a man who would rescue his kidnapped daughters. The boy was about to volunteer when he woke up, and he realized that it had all been a dream—a very strange dream. He worked just as hard the second day as he did the day before. The smith's daughter took pity on him and gave him some food in secret, just enough so he wouldn't starve. The blacksmith was surprised. As he was evil, he had intended to work the boy to death. When the year was over—for back then three days made up a year – and the was fence finished, the smith asked the apprentice what he wanted for his service. The boy asked for time to consider the question and went to the garden to meet with the smith's daughter. "Don't ask for anything. Let him give you whatever he wants. You will be better off that way," she suggested.

But the boy was greedy, and he wanted to be paid for all the hard work he had done. He asked for gold. The smith realized that the boy did not know any better, so he gave him a large piece of gold wrapped in a handkerchief. The boy left happily, never looking back, imagining how his mother would not have to do laundry anymore. But as he walked out the door and unwrapped the bundle to admire the gold in the sunlight, it turned into a plain rock right in front of his eyes. Furious, he threw it to the ground and marched off into the wide world. No one ever saw him again.

Sometime later, the mother sent out her second son. She warned him to be smarter than his brother. The boy set out, and when he became hungry, he sat down under a tree to eat his ash cake. As he was eating, a little lizard crawled onto his hand and asked for a morsel. The boy told him he barely had any and chased the lizard away.

The next morning, the second son reached the city. There he apprenticed himself to a cooper, a barrel-maker. The cooper told him there was a lot of work to do for the King had ordered a wine barrel large enough to hold the yield from an entire mountainside vineyard. He hired the boy as an apprentice on the spot. They set to work, drilled and carved all day, but the boy got nothing to eat. Occasionally, the master would eat a piece of sausage or a piece of bread from his apron pocket. There was also a flask in the workshop, which the cooper sometimes took a swig from. But he offered neither food nor drink to the boy. Falling asleep on his cot that night, the apprentice had a dream. He was at a royal feast and whatever he lifted to his mouth, be it roasted or cooked meat, it all turned into lizards that skittered away with a mocking laugh.

This boy also fell in love with his master's daughter. She told him that when his apprentice time ended, he should leave the payment arrangements to her father. The boy, however, had his eyes on the flask, which he had been admiring from a distance. He asked for it as compensation for his work. The cooper resisted at first, saying that it was almost empty and not worth much, but gave in at the end. The girl warned the boy not to open the flask until he arrived home, but he was thirsty. The moment he stepped out of the city, he opened the flask and took a swig. It was filled with poison, and the boy fell dead. He was buried there by the road, and his mother never saw him again.

The mother told her youngest son never to leave her alone, and he stayed home until she died. He buried her, planted a maple tree on her grave, and then set out to seek his fortune. He had no ash cakes, only a small hatchet. Cutting himself a strong walking stick, he walked and walked and walked until he arrived at a great city. It was the city where the King lived, the same King who had ordered the fence and the giant barrel. The boy went to court and greeted him politely.

"May God give you a good evening, my Royal Father?"

"May He give the same to you, poor lad. What is your business here?"

"I am seeking service."

The King was happy to hear that. He had been looking for a new guard for his vineyard because the old one had been taken by the Devil. The King and the boy made a deal. If the boy guarded the grapes well until harvest, he could ask for whatever he wished. He took his hatchet, got a satchel full of food from the royal kitchen, and asked the servants to point out the road that led to the vineyards. He walked and walked until he came across a beautiful tree with branches all the way down to the ground. As he looked at the bright green leaves, he noticed a little ant stuck to one of them. He peeled it off and carefully set it free on the ground.

"I can see you are kinder than your brother was," said the ant. "I will help you. Here is this pin, stick it into your hat, and if you need me, just pull it out. I'll be there right away."

The boy thanked him with a smile and put the pin away. As he walked around the tree, he noticed that there was a ladder propped up against it. He climbed the ladder and continued climbing from branch to branch. Even though he climbed all day, he was only halfway up when night fell. He lay down on a giant leaf, swayed gently in the evening breeze, watched the moon rise, and then fell asleep. The next morning, he continued his climb. As he was cutting a new handhold into the bark with his hatchet, he noticed a little lizard stuck to the tree in a patch of resin. He peeled the tiny creature off very carefully, and set it free.

The lizard spoke, "You have been kind to me, unlike your brother, so I will be kind to you. If you need help, just take out this piece of skin, and I will come to you."

The boy thanked the lizard, tucked the piece of skin into his pocket, and continued climbing. Only a little farther up, he heard the screeching of a falcon trapped in a tangle of branches. He carefully bent and twisted the branches until the bird's wings were freed.

"Thank you for your kindness," the falcon said. "I will repay it one day. Take this feather from my tail and use it to call me when you need help."

The boy tucked the feather into his hat and continued climbing.

By the time night fell, he found himself in a beautiful vineyard. It was surrounded by a wire fence so tightly woven that not even a mosquito could slip through. And yet, as he walked among the vines, he noticed that invisible hands were stealing the grapes. He took out his hatchet and threw it in their direction. There came a cry, a yell, and a pained voice promising not to steal anymore. The boy put the hatchet back on his belt with a satisfied smile.

Days passed. Three days was a year back then, and the grapes were ripening nicely under the boy's careful watch. On the third morning, he heard a commotion. As he looked around, he saw the King walking towards him with his entire court, dressed for labor and ready to harvest.

"You have been very brave, my boy. While we harvest the grapes, I have another job for you. You shall be guarding my pigs and taking them to pasture."

The court began to harvest the grapes into the great barrel the cooper had made. While they did so, the boy herded the pigs (yes, there was also a pasture on top of the magic tree). But lo and behold, the moment the pigs reached the field they all burrowed underground and disappeared. The boy was desperate, having thought that guarding pigs would be an easier job than it proved to be. As he mourned the loss, he scratched his head. His hand found the pin in his hat and, as soon as the pulled it out, the ant was right in front of him.

“What is your wish, my darling master?”

The boy told the ant that he was tasked with guarding the King’s pigs, and they had all disappeared underground.

“Don’t worry, master, they are not really pigs. They are the King’s daughters.”

“The King’s daughters?! How would I not worry?! Now he will have me executed for sure!”

“You will live, I promise. I’ll go after the pigs and herd them back. When they come your way, throw this handful of barley at them, and they will follow your every command.”

And so it happened. The pigs surfaced, snorting and squealing as ants bit their haunches. The boy threw barley at them, and they were instantly tamed. One of them, a little spotted pig, especially seemed to like the boy. As they walked home in the evening, he picked up the little pig and cradled her in his arms.

The next morning, the swineherd, for that was his official occupation now, took the pigs to the pasture again. The moment they got there, all the pigs ran to a stream, plopped into the water, and sank out of sight. The boy pulled out the lizard skin hoping he would receive help.

“What is your wish, my dear master?”

A few moments later, having heard what happened, the tiny creature was already herding the pigs out of the water. The swineherd, as he was told, threw a handful of corn at them. They spent the rest of the day around him, peaceful and happily snorting. Once again, he carried the spotted piglet home in his arms.

On the third morning, the King called for the swineherd.

“Listen, my boy, if you and I both survive this day, we will be happy forever. Today is the day the curse on my daughters must be broken. It was going to last until we had a full harvest of golden grapes, and if we kept the pigs from running away. The grapes have been harvested, and the pigs are still here… all thanks to you. Every year before you came to my court, the grapes were stolen by devils and the pigs scattered every which way.”

The boy told the King about the ant, the lizard, and the falcon. The King could see that he was kind-hearted, with strength in his arm, and a mother's blessing. He wished him good luck on his last day as a swineherd, for himself and for the good of the entire kingdom.

The swineherd led the pigs to the pasture. The moment they arrived, they broke free, squealing as they all suddenly rose into the air, bobbing up higher and higher, until they disappeared above the clouds. The boy chose to use his last chance, and picked the feather out of his hat. In that moment, the falcon swooped down from the sky and herded the buoyant pigs down to the ground where the swineherd waited for them with a handful of wheat. The third debt was thus repaid.

That evening, when the boy returned home carrying the spotted piglet in his arms, the King said to him, "My son—for you are my son from now on—what payment do you wish?"

The boy blushed at the kind words.

"I would like to keep this piglet, my Royal Father. And I would like to keep serving you, if you please."

The King laughed the way the Devils used to laugh before they all got locked up in the giant barrel with the grapes.

"Toss that scrawny pig away, and I'll give you the largest, fattest mother sow I own."

But the boy teared up and cradled the piglet to his chest. As he did, it turned back into the King's most beloved daughter, so beautiful even the sun paused on its journey to look at her. The King hugged his daughter and hugged the swineherd, whose kindness and loyalty had saved them all. He gave the young couple everything he had: the kingdom, the tree, and the barrel.

They had a splendid wedding. They would have opened the barrel, too, to drink some golden wine, but everyone was afraid of the Devils trapped inside. Finally, the brave little swineherd tapped it, the Devils leaked out and fled in every direction. If the Devils had not fled, my story might have lasted longer.

## Comments

This story bears many similarities with folktales that fall into the "Tree that grows up to the sky" type and exist in many European traditions, including Rusyn, Slovakian, Romanian, Roma, Jewish, and Hungarian (ATU 317). Furicz János also had a version of it. The magic tree, sometimes also called Sky-high Tree, or Tree Without a Top, serves as a ladder into a magical world. The first two brothers, following the rules of folktales, fail at finding their fortune. But in this case, the results of their work provide help for the swineherd to accomplish his tasks and save the kingdom. Originally, the King ordered a mere twenty meters of fence, which would hardly be enough for a vineyard, so I changed it to two hundred.

The Princesses who have been turned into animals and must be herded back home with the help of kind creatures are also a motif that frequently appears in Hungarian tradition. Sometimes they are lambs or horses rather than pigs, but I liked the subtle humor in Anna's depiction of them. In many traditional tales, events repeat three times. In the original text of this story, the third crisis—along with the helping animal, possibly a bird to add the element of Air to the ant's Earth and the lizard's Water—seems to have been lost, allowing the swineherd to simply walk to pasture and then back home on the third day. When I tell the story, I add the falcon and the buoyant pigs to round out the triple structure.

I cannot explain why the mother's beatings are so elaborately described at the beginning of the story since they don't seem to have a direct effect on the rest of the events. My first instinct was to cut that part, but I decided against it, leaving the decision in future storytellers' hands. I would also like to note that the boy sleeping on a leaf, watching the moonlight, is not a detail I added – it was in Anna's original story and I found it a very vivid image.

Ash cakes, usually made by the mother, are a staple food in Hungarian folktales for heroes setting out to seek their fortune. They are a form of pastry made from flour, salt, and water and baked in the hot ashes of the fireplace.

# Part Three

## Questions Big and Small

Hungarian folktales don't usually have titles. In the oral tradition, they begin with an opening formula, or they are prompted with the name of the hero, or a hint about their most exciting feat, by members of the audience who have already heard them and want to hear them again. Most titles are a handle for organizing texts in a written format and providing an appealing Table of Contents for story collections.

When I was reading through Pályuk Anna's repertoire in the Archives, I noticed that quite a few of her stories were titled with questions. Some are great, even cosmic, almost philosophical questions ("Who owns the moonlight?" "Why are there no fairies in the world?"). Others sound like eager prompts from dedicated listeners ("What did the piglet do in the winter?"). I can't tell if these titles were invented by Anna, or the collector, or simply lifted from conversations that happened between stories. Still, there were enough of them to merit their own chapter. So now, at the halfway point of the book, I offer you some vast, timeless questions that are best answered in story.

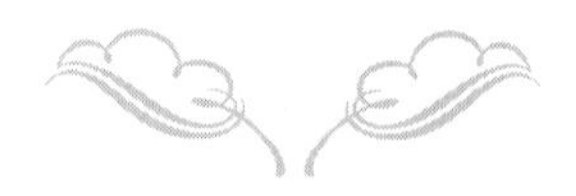

# Who Owns the Moonlight?

A long, long time ago, when it was not yet known that moonlight is free for everyone, an argument broke out over who owns it. Humans said it was theirs, and animals said it was theirs. They couldn't agree. The disagreement went on and on for two or three thousand years. Finally, a man, who was a kind of scientist, suggested that the moonlight should belong to *everyone who enjoys it.*

"How can that be?" protested another man. "I go to sleep in the evening and wake up in the morning. I save the moonlight; I only enjoy it occasionally, so it doesn't run out."

Animals countered saying that they didn't look at all; they simply *allowed* it to shine on them. Therefore, they were doing a better job at preserving moonlight than the humans. The debate continued until they finally decided to send some humans and some animals up to the Moon with a written inquiry, asking directly to whom it wanted to belong. But on the night they wanted to set out, there was no moon in the sky. It was on the other side of the earth, and the night was pitch dark. People and animals both concluded it was not a good time to leave. In the darkness, they would surely fall into a ditch. Then whoever owned the moonlight would not be them, so they kept on arguing and stayed home until the new Moon appeared.

Once they had their eyes on their goal again, they set out together. The delegation walked for three weeks, but couldn't reach the Moon. Then it got dark again, so dark they couldn't see their hands in front of their faces. Everyone, humans and animals, stumbled over each other on the road.

A man came up with a suggestion.

"Listen friends, no one can win this way. Let's stop wandering around here in the middle of nowhere. The Moon is clearly playing hide and seek with u. We will never reach it and never go home unless we agree on something. So, let us agree that whoever sees the Moon first will own its light forever."

All animals and humans agreed, and they began their journey towards home. They were at the edge of their village when they spotted the Moon rising over the church tower, right in front of them. They immediately began to argue again—who saw it first? They noticed a young couple walking by the tower hand in hand, singing happily.

"Let's ask them. They must know."

Animals looked around, too, and noticed two cats sitting on the church roof, singing in their own language. So, they called them down.

They asked the two couples, the humans and the cats side by side, "Who owns the moonlight?"

And all four of them answered at once as if they had rehearsed it, "The moonlight belongs to the young!"

Since they all said the same thing, there was no more debate. It was decided that the moonlight belongs to the young.

It is amusing to see old people enjoying the moonlight. Even three thousand years ago, it belonged to the young, and so it does today. Of course, that doesn't mean that old people can't look at it occasionally, too.

When my father told this story, he asked the people around him, "What do *you* think?"

And everyone answered that they must have known it three thousand years ago – if it belonged to the young then, so it does now. We old people only watch it a little bit, now and then, since we also need warmth with the light. However beautiful the Moon is, it doesn't warm you one bit. Uncle Gyuri puts on a fur coat whenever he wants to look at it.

## Comments

Sometimes when I tell this story, especially on occasions with a theme that involves love, I tell it as "The moonlight belongs to those in love." As short and simple as it is, it stretches especially well, and allows a playful space for the audience to ask the questions: Who does the moonlight belong to? How should the question be decided? Who appreciates the moonlight more?

In addition, the story also follows the phases of the moon. With a little tweaking, it works great as a classroom story. I was once asked by a little girl, "But what about nocturnal animals?"

The "fur coat" in question is a *suba*, a cloak-like garment made from wooly sheep-skin. It was commonly used by people, especially shepherds, who wanted to stay warm while sleeping under the stars. I left it in, together with Anna's own account of her father's telling, because it gives us a glimpse into the original context of these stories and the exchanges that happened between teller and audience.

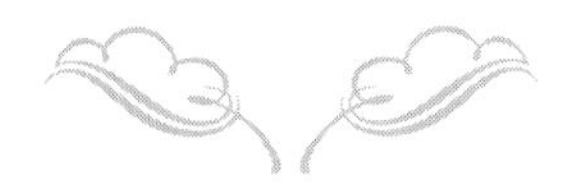

# What is the Wind Called?

In the olden days, no one knew what turned the hay bales on the fields upside down and scattered them every which way. This mysterious force sometimes tore up trees, too, or pushed people into a crevice even if they were clinging to something. What could it be? People got smarter with time and, eventually, they concluded that it was *not* a witch or a monster. It was something coming from above that was not summoned and not sent, but came and went of its own accord.

But what could it be? And what was it called?

One day, a shepherd was tending his sheep on the mountainside. Not a leaf moved, and the sun was shining brightly. Suddenly something, some invisible power, scared the sheep, and they scattered in all directions. Almost half the flock was lost. The shepherd and his friends were baffled. They hadn't seen anything. Yet, the sheep were running, so terrified of something that they almost broke their legs. What could it be? As the six shepherds and a clerk were counting the remaining flock, the invisible force suddenly shoved them to the side. The shepherds stuck their staffs into the ground, braced themselves, and waited for the appearance of whatever creature was causing it. They waited in vain.

The clerk, dusting himself off, finally said, "Listen, I will go tell the landlord what happened. We need to find out what, or who, is behind all this."

The clerk went to the village. There he saw, in great shock, that the houses were all damaged. Some had lost their roofs, while others lost their front or their back walls.

"What could cause such damage?" he wondered as he walked down the street. Soon he ran into the village judge.

"Do you see what happened to the village?!" the judge asked.

"I do, but I can't tell what caused it," answered the clerk.

"We can't either. It came from above, but no one knows what it is. There is an old copper-working Gypsy at the end of the street. He has wandered all over the world and is a very knowledgeable man. He must know the answer. I am on my way to ask him. Come with me if you want."

They went together to the old Gypsy. They found him patching up his cottage.

"Listen, Dádé, what was it that did so much damage in the village?"

The old man looked at the judge and the clerk, who had never come out in person to see him before, and decided to make money out of his answer. He told them the Devil would surely take him if he revealed it.

"And if you don't, *we* will take you!" the judge snapped. "Which one would you rather choose?"

"Very well. I will tell you for a piglet. If it's half dead, that's okay, too. There are many of those in the village right now."

"You can have two. If you answer our question," said the judge.

"Very well, very good, I will tell you right now... With respect, gentlemen, the thing that broke the houses and scattered the sheep was the Soul of the Mountains!"

"The mountains have a soul?" chimed in the priest, who had just caught up to the group and wanted to join the conversation.

"Of course, they do, father, and what a soul it is! If it is angered, not even the babes will survive. But when it is in a good mood, it will stroke and caress you like a woman's hand, and you know those well, judge sir, clerk sir, father... am I right?"

"How on earth would I know?!" protested the priest, but the judge and the clerk only smirked. They knew.

They all set out for home, resolved in knowing that it was the Soul of the Mountains doing all the damage. They thought that if the mountains had such a wrathful soul, it had to be defeated somehow. On the way home, they met a man soaked to the bone and stumbling around.

"Where do you come from, friend?" asked the priest.

"I am coming from the plains. We had such foul weather that man and animal barely stayed alive!"

They all thought at once: *It is not the Soul of the Mountains, after all! It could not do such damage on the plains.*

They asked the man, "Do you know what it is called… the thing that destroyed everything?"

"How would I know, it didn't introduce itself! It came suddenly, and it went the same way. It must have been a great and powerful lord for it ruined a lot of poor people's lives."

The four men decided to seek answers in the city. They set out together. As they were walking along the road, they noticed a rickety cart ahead of them, drawn not by horses, but by two ugly kittens! *What can this be,* their eyes asked, as they looked at each other. As they got closer, they saw a large bag in the back of the cart, heaving, moving, straining. *What can this carriage be transporting?* The clerk was dying of curiosity, so he caught up to the cart, reached in, and untied the bag. Doing so was a bad idea. In a moment, that mysterious, powerful thing that had done all the damage was right on top of them! He hastily tied the bag shut again and then ran around to the front of the carriage to talk to its owner.

The owner was a cloud!

After a lengthy pause, they mustered up the courage and the courtesy to ask the cloud ever so politely if it would tell them what was in the bag.

The cloud let out a laugh, ignoring their pleas, and yelled into the air, "The wind! The wind!"

"I don't understand. What is he yelling?" asked the priest, confused.

But the clerk understood. "Wind" was the name of that mysterious force.

"This is what that power is called that treated us so roughly. The wind. That's its name. Wind."

They soon made up some other names for it, too: Storm, gale, whirlwind, tempest, breeze... And ever since then, we have been using the same words whenever that mysterious force makes an appearance.

**Comments**

Winds and storms are cruel in the Carpathians. Anna talks about the wind as something that comes from "above," from the mountains, destroying things with unstoppable force. It plays an important part in several of her tales. One that gave its title to an entire story collection tells about the *Goddaughter of Auntie Wind* (*Szélanyó keresztlánya*), an old woman who lives alone except for the Wind visiting her, dancing with her, and helping her with her chores. In another story, a boy who sets out to seek his fortune travels with the Wind around the world. There is a mythical, symbolic quality to these tales, with the wind having several different, distinct personalities, both male and female. The way the clerk accidentally releases the wind from the bag in this story is reminiscent of a similar scene in the *Odyssey,* and is known around the world in many cultures (Thompson Motif Index, C322.1). There is a Rusyn folktale, a version of the *Twelve-Month Brothers*, where a poor man is rewarded by Wind, Frost, and Rain for finding something good in all of them; and there is also a Slovakian one where the hero visits the palaces of the Kings of Water, Fire, Wind, and Time (this last one on top of the Glass Mountain).

*Szél* is the Hungarian word used for "wind" and the elusive name sought in this story. *Dádé,* in this case, is not the old man's name – it is the vocative form of the Romani word for "father," usually used when addressing elders.

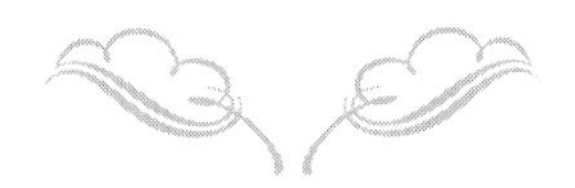

# Why Are There No Fairies in the World?

This is a big question, almost too big for one's mind. Many people tried to answer it, but no one succeeded. I thought about it a lot, too, when I was young. One day, a traveling man told me that there was a small cottage at the foot of the mountains in which lived a hundred-year-old woman who knew everything. I decided to go and ask her: *Why are there no fairies in the world?*

I made ready for the journey. My mother, who was getting old, kept telling me to stay. She said that there was no use in going because no one could answer that question. But believe it or not, I set out anyway with my distaff in my hand, two spindles and two small biscuits in my bag. I walked and walked, up one mountain and down another.

I must have been close to the edge of the world when suddenly a little man sprang up in front of me and said, "Anica, where are you going? What are you carrying? Who are you working for?"

I was stunned. How did the little old man know who I was? I didn't show fear.

I answered, "I am looking for someone who can tell me why there are no fairies in the world!"

"Oh, Anica, Anica, you don't even know that much? You don't have to go any farther. I can tell you... if you spin that flax for me and give me your biscuits."

It was not a high price, so I agreed to the bargain. I knew I had to keep it, it was only fair, so I gave him the food. As he sat down on a milestone to eat, I leaned against a nearby tree and began spinning very fast. I waited patiently for him to tell me why there are no fairies in the world. Then when I was about to prompt him, he finally began to talk.

"Do you know, Anica, why there are no fairies in the world? When I was still a child, like you are now, my mother told me that an evil fairy killed all the boys. When there were both boys and girls in the house, the evil fairy killed the girls, too. There were houses where she killed eight or ten children in one night. At first, people didn't know what or who was killing the children. They finally found out because the evil fairy went to the wrong place – the night guard's house. The night guard was about to leave so he could call midnight in the village when he saw a beautiful woman fly in through the window. It was summer, you see, and very hot. The windows were open, like in every other house in the village. As the night guard watched, wondering what she wanted, the evil fairy sat on the chest of his sleeping son, and squeezed the little boy's neck. The boy died immediately. The evil fairy let out a cruel laugh and was about to fly out the window, but the father was quicker. He grabbed her by the skirt and struggled with her until he managed to squeeze her neck in the same way. She died just like the boy.

In the morning, when the night guard told his wife what happened, she ran straight to the priest to have him say prayers for the souls of the dead. The priest came to the house and recognized immediately that the beautiful woman was a fairy. He concluded that if she was, then all those children must have been killed by fairies as well. Therefore, the evil creatures had to be wiped from the face of the earth. People agreed. They all went out and combed through the forests, meadows, and mountains. Wherever they found a fairy, they killed it. If you don't believe me, find the priest and ask him. This is how I know it, and believe me, it is true. This is why there are no more fairies in the world."

By the time he finished, I had spun both spools full. He took the spools and walked away. I stood there watching him go. Soon he disappeared, and I don't know where he went. I was sad that he didn't tell me more stories, but since I now had the answer to my question, I walked back home.

When I got back to the house, my mother was waiting for me at the door with two bolts of linen. She said that a man had left them for me. He insisted they were mine, even though my mother told him I had never worked for a shopkeeper or a factory. He didn't say much else. We made pretty petticoats and blouses from the linen for me.

I spun that thread. He wove it. This is the end of my story.

**Comments**

There are only two tales in Anna's repertoire that she told in the first person – and this is the only one that also involves a hint of the supernatural. I translated it as close to the original wording as possible because I think part of the magic of this tale is that it's so simple. Yet, it has such a powerful, lingering conclusion told in a serious and matter-of-fact tone. How could someone make two bolts of linen from the yarn that had only been spun shortly before? Who—or *what*—was that little old man?

Fairies (*tündér, tündérek*) in Hungarian folk belief, and even in tales, are not always benevolent creatures. The evil kind of fairy woman mentioned in this tale shares some features with night hags and wraiths (*lidérc*), for she suffocates children by sitting on their chest. In Hungarian folklore, fairies are sometimes also responsible for changelings, although our changeling lore is not nearly as diverse or developed as the Celtic traditions. The word often used for malevolent fairy women is *szépasszony* ("beautiful woman"). They were feared for their abilities to cause suffering and misery.

There are other stories in the Hungarian tradition that recount how and why the fairies left this world. In some, they do so on their own volition because of people's cruel ways. Sometimes they do so because they can't stand the sound of church bells or they run out of water and people don't give them any. In a story from my home region, Szigetköz, one of them turns into a water lily and continues keeping watch over humanity. However, I have never encountered another tale where fairies are systematically hunted to (near?) extinction.

A night guard (*bakter*, from the German *Wächter*) was a man responsible for patrolling villages and towns at night and calling out the hours. It is important that the fairy visits his house because he is awake to see her do the horrible deed. What I translated as "biscuits" is a kind of cornmeal bun (*málécipó*).

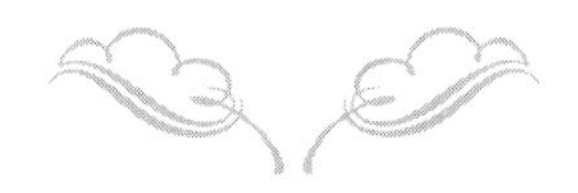

# Who Owns the Golden Apples?

Once upon a time, very far away, a skip and a hop beyond the edge of the world, there was a beautiful garden. In that garden grew apples that shone at night with a bright, golden light. Mortals never tasted them. Angels frequented the garden to snack, and sometimes a young devil or two would steal a bagful of the magic fruit.

But one day, trouble came to the garden when mortals got a craving for a taste of the apples. They not only wanted the apples, but they also wanted the whole garden for themselves! But they could not get in, for an angel with a flaming sword guarded the gates. It was a fearsome guardian, much stronger than the average gardener. The mortals, however, didn't give up. They picked up their axes, pickaxes, and shovels, and attacked the angel. Numbers won, and the mortals managed to beat down the guardian. That evening, in the cool sunset, the angels came to eat apples, but instead, they found their guardian in a sorry state. He lay face down under a large tree, moaning in pain from the beating the mortals had given him. Meanwhile, the gates had been left wide open.

The ownership of the golden apples had to be decided. The angels fluttered this way and that until finally a clever little angel went to an old lawyer and told him everything. He told the lawyer that, ever since the dawn of memory, the angels had owned the golden apples. Now that the mortals had found them, they didn't want to give them back. The guardian had been beaten badly, and justice was needed. The old lawyer offered no advice for he was mortal, too, and he sided with the mortals.

The angels wanted the garden back. They liked the apples. What would they snack on if the apples were gone? So, the Little Angel went to a young and learned lawyer, one that still believed in justice, and told him how their apple guardian had been beaten by mortals.

"This is bad business," said the young lawyer, even though he was a mortal himself. "Beating up someone who is protecting their own is intolerable. Just wait! I will make sure that the mortals pay for what they have done."

The Little Angel liked the promise so much that he gave three shining stars to the lawyer as an advance payment. The lawyer was very happy. He took them home to his wife, who was sick and lying in bed. He thought, *If the angels pay so well, I am willing to take all their cases.*

Mortals and angels were summoned for a grand trial. But neither side presented any witnesses.

"I can't decide things this way," complained the judge. The mortals' case was stronger than the angels' case because their lawyer was the old one who knew all the tricks of the trade.

The judge declared his decision, "Whoever brings the better witness, will get the golden apples."

With no other options left, the angels' young lawyer called the Devil as their witness. He had stolen from the garden often enough that he must have seen something! On the other side, the mortals called the Moonlight as a witness. The old lawyer got the Moon to swear that it had seen mortals tend the garden at night. Therefore, they had the right to eat the apples, too. As for the Devil, the old lawyer insisted that he could not be a witness for he was a thief and a notorious liar.

The trial dragged on and on, and then it took a sudden, unexpected turn. One night, a storm blew in and knocked all the apples out of the trees. Now the angels were in trouble. What to do with all the fallen fruit? They had no pigs to feed. Since the apples would have gone to waste, the judge ruled in favor of the mortals, who owned pigs.

The mortals were satisfied, but not for long. The storm was followed by a dry, hot wind, which shrunk the apples to the size of walnuts. No one wanted them, not even the pigs. Who would clean them up? Believe it or not, there was still someone who made a claim. The Devil arrived with a cart and took all the dry apples away as fire fodder for Hell. The dried apples burned well, you see.

So in the end, neither the angels nor the mortals had any golden apples. You should not bicker over things because the Devil will take them. By the next year, the angels and the mortals had made a compromise to share the garden. When my great-grandfather was there, they were harvesting together. He got three apples and planted their seeds. We still have golden apples growing in our very own garden. I don't like them, though, they are too sour and too small to bite. It is said that the apples became like that from all the bickering. Believe it or don't, that's all I know. But look at these apples now, was it worth it to argue that much?

**Comments**

What Anna calls "golden apple" (*aranyalma*) in this pseudo-Biblical courtroom drama is a kind of small, yellow fruit, most likely a Chinese apple or crabapple. My own grandparents grow them in their orchard, too. They are indeed sour, and hard to bite. "Shrunk to the size of walnuts" is originally "shrunk to the size of galls" (*gubacs*), growths often found on plants.

There is an entire collection of Hungarian folktales that are based on Biblical themes; it is aptly named *Parasztbiblia*, *The Peasant Bible*. This tale, as amusing as it is vivid, brings angels and mortals into the same courtroom to contest the ownership of the apples from the Garden (of Eden), until the Devil, the usual laughing third party, takes them all. This story works both as a cautionary tale and an origin story; maybe better as the latter, since the "pointless bickering" began with a bunch of intruders beating up the Angel of the Flaming Sword.

The Hungarian language does not have gendered pronouns, so the angels in the story could be any gender (or genderless). In English, the choice is up to the storyteller.

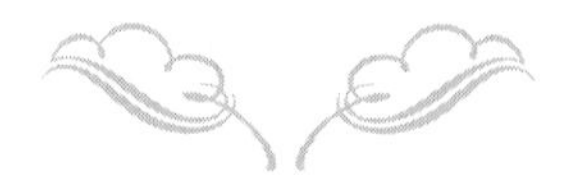

# Where Did the Son of the White Mare Go?

Once upon a time, on a faraway mountain, there was a pasture. On that pasture lived horses so beautiful that every king selected his stallion from among them. And even among these horses, the most beautiful was the White Mare. Rumor claimed that her mother had been a *táltos,* faster than the wind, faster than thought. This White Mare had a colt so beautiful that the sun went around the pasture three times every day just to watch him run. When he ran, his hooves kicked up sparks as if he had been running on diamonds. If it were not for these sparks, anyone watching would have thought his hooves never touched the ground. The owner of the stables never wanted to sell him to anyone. He hoped that he would have a son one day, and the son would get the beautiful white colt for his first birthday.

But it didn't happen that way.

One day, a King passed by the pasture and saw the white colt. The moment he saw it, he wanted to own it. I don't know how much he offered, but it must have been a fortune because the owner sold the colt. The White Mare mourned the loss of her son. She saw danger in his future, and she was right.

The King that bought the colt was soon challenged to war by the King of the Saracens. He took the white horse with him to the battlefield. The horse shone so brightly that he had to be concealed somehow or the enemy would easily pick out the King riding him. The court painter painted the colt black from nose to tail, so that even his own mother would not have recognized him. It was tedious work, for the horse had to be re-painted every morning after he rubbed off the black paint in the stables. Homesick, and fed up with the stinking paint on his coat, he decided to run away. But it was not as easily done as thought, for guards who stood everywhere herded the horse back to the stables every time he broke free. Finally, on a stormy night, he managed to slip away and ran as fast as his legs could carry him, kicking up sparks wherever he went.

When dawn came, he realized that he was standing right at the edge of a dangerous precipice. One moment he was relieved he had not fallen. At the next moment, the ground gave way under his hooves, and he was tumbling down, down, down. When he finally skidded to a halt, he felt something burning his legs. *Where am I,* he wondered? But he already suspected the answer. He had fallen straight into Hell. *I will never escape from here alive*, he thought.

As he looked around, he noticed a group of small children chasing each other on top of the smoldering embers. There were more children than he could count. The horse wondered how the embers did not burn them. It took some time for him to realize that they were little devils and not mortal children. They could not burn, but the horse could, and the searing heat hurt him badly. His tongue lolled out from thirst and pain. Finally, he spotted a ditch full of water, ran straight to it to escape the flames, and threw himself into the middle with a splash.

It was the river that divided Heaven from Hell, filled with milk taken from witches when they asked to be allowed into Heaven. Since one shore was Hell, the milk was boiling. It almost cooked the son of the White Mare alive. He barely managed to scramble out on the other side.

When he did, he saw an old man and a bundle of winged children staring at him. The old man was Saint Peter himself, Guardian of Heaven. The winged children were angels.

When they saw the horse smeared with dirt and ashes, they caught him, and the Saint said, "If you were a pure white horse, you could stay here, live with us, and carry messages for us. But since you are neither black nor white, you cannot stay."

The horse whinnied, explaining that he had been pure white, but the King that took him to war had painted him black; his coat remained stained even after all the adventures. At that, Saint Peter ordered the angels to wash him and rub him down. Washed, the horse turned pure white again, more beautiful and shining than he had ever been. Saint Peter fed him, the angels brought him cool water, and he soon regained his strength. He ran, neighed, and played with the little angels – most often with a black-haired boy among them. Saint Peter noticed, and so did the others. I will tell you why. The black-haired boy was the son of the White Mare's owner. He was the one that the white colt had been destined for, once upon a time. The horse and the boy spent endless days reminiscing about their home, the pasture, the farmer, and the horses. One day, the white horse came to a decision.

"Listen, little one, I have decided that I will go home to my mother or die trying. If you would like to come along, I will take you, too."

"No one has ever tried to escape from Heaven, but if you believe you can do it, dear white horse, I will go with you."

So they talked on a moonlit night. When all the angels went to sleep, the little black-haired one stayed out. Whether no one noticed or no one called him out, I don't know; but he stayed out, put a bridle on the white horse, threw a blanket from one of the beds onto his back, and they took their leave of Heaven. They began their journey down the Milky Way. They knew that other people on horseback had used that road before them; it was easy enough to follow.

By the morning, they found themselves in a large forest. Neither of them knew what corner of the world they had landed in, or in which direction they needed to continue their journey home. Looking around for clues, they noticed a small house. The black-haired angel knocked on the door, and when an old woman opened it, he inquired politely to whom the forest belonged.

"You must come from very far away if you don't know," said the woman, wrinkles rippling on her face.

"We come from Heaven," said the white horse.

"Bones and cabbages, that is indeed very far!"

"Could you tell us who owns this forest, please?"

"You were honest with me, so I will tell you. This forest belongs to the man who owns the finest horses in all the land. But he is very sad now because he sold the most beautiful of them all, the white colt, and his little black-haired son died before he could have been baptized. He has no joy left in this world."

"We will bring him joy, grandmother."

"Oh, if you would, I would become young again, too. I was his wife's first maid, but in a house so full of sorrow and tears, everyone ages twice as fast. So, did I."

The white horse nudged the boy gently.

"Let us go, little angel, and find my mother and your father."

They arrived home together, the angel riding on the back of the white horse. They came to the pasture first. All the horses gathered around them, neighing in excitement.

"Where have you been?" they asked.

When the white colt told them about his journey, they pranced with joy. One ran to the corrals to bring the news to the White Mare, who had been standing there with her head hanging low even since her son left. She could barely stand, but in the next moment, her white colt was already at her side, and they hugged each other like people do. The black-haired little angel went inside the house to see his mother and father, who at first thought they were dreaming. But it was not a dream, it was all real. The boy had come back from Heaven, and he promised to stay. Back in the war, the white colt had visited the Fountain of Life with the King and had kept a bottle of its waters in his saddlebags. Now he sprinkled it on himself and on the boy, and they were as alive and as real as ever.

Joy filled the house, and it overflowed to the pasture. This was the story of the white horse's journey.

**Comments**

The folktale that is probably the most well-known among all Hungarian tales bears a very similar title to this one: It is called *Fehérlófia*, Son of the White Mare. In that story, the son is human, a hero possessing supernatural strength. The image is so commonly known that I was surprised when I first read this text and it turned out to be about *actual horses*.

There is an underlying narrative in this story, which is that of a child who dies before being baptized. It is hard to tell if this happens after the colt is sold or if his owner sells him because there is no boy to gift him to anymore. Colt and boy clearly belong together and find each other on the far side of death. There is extensive lore in the Hungarian tradition about child mortality. In many cases, unbaptized children become ghosts or can't enter Heaven. While the story states that both horse and angels are *in* Heaven, we also first see the children playing outside, in the company of Saint Peter, just at the edge of the river between Heaven and Hell. They seem to have a marginal place in the afterworld. The river of boiling milk, by the way, is a very vivid image The storyteller's claim that it is the "milk taken from witches that asked to go into Heaven" refers to a belief I did not manage to track down.

*T*áltos is a word commonly used in folktales for a magic horse; it has shamanistic connotations (see *The Daughter of the Táltos King* in the last chapter). The comment about how "other riders" used the Milky Way is an amazingly subtle hint at the legend of Prince Csaba, an old Hungarian tradition that claims that Attila the Hun's son and his warriors left that path of sparks on the sky when they returned from beyond the grave to help the *Székely* people on the battlefield. Because of this story, the Milky Way is also known as *Hadak Útja*, the Road of the Warriors.

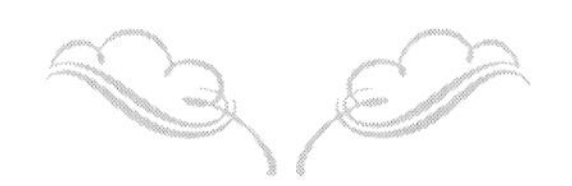

# What Did the Little Pig Do in the Winter?

Once upon a time, there was a great big forest and, in the middle of the forest, there was a neat little house. In the house lived an old man with his pig. He loved that pig as if it had been his child. He talked to the pig as if it had been human. And, believe it or not, the pig understood every single word he said. They walked the forest together, the old man gathering berries and the pig eating acorns. The pig sometimes found and dug up mushrooms, then dragged the old man, by the tobacco pouch hanging from the old man's belt, to the mushrooms. They lived like that during the summer and the fall, sharing their days and sharing their food.

But in the winter, there were no mushrooms or berries. There were acorns because the old man had gathered a lot, but, even with that, they did not have much to eat. The pig felt sorry for its human, so it set out to find some food. He routed this way and that, but the snow was so deep it came up to its belly, and the pig found nothing edible. The next day it set out even earlier to search deeper in the forest.

Waddling along in the snow, the pig was spotted by a great shaggy wolf. The wolf was happy to see food coming his way for he had not eaten in weeks. The moment the pig spotted the wolf, it squealed and burrowed in a pile of snow so deep not even its tail poked out. The wolf sat down to wait. The pig had to come out sometime! The wolf didn't see it happen, however, because a hunter passed by and killed the wolf. The pig heard the commotion and knew that it was now safe to come out. While he had been hiding in the pile of snow – or rather, the pile of leaves under it – he noticed the smell of mushrooms. The pile was full of them! The pig ran home, grabbed the old man's tobacco pouch in its teeth, and dragged him into the forest. *This pig never pulls me like this unless it found mushrooms*, the old man thought and followed along. When they came to the pile of snow, the old man poked at it with a pitchfork (he always carried a pitchfork in the woods). He was overjoyed to turn up mushrooms as large as half a hat each. *If mushrooms survive in the winter like this, I will build some piles next year*, he thought. He covered the pile again, took some mushrooms home every day, and left the rest cool and fresh under the snow. Now they had something to eat.

Water was also scarce in the winter. The old man had to boil snow to drink. The piglet decided to find a better water source, one that was not frozen solid. However, it ran into trouble once again when a bear noticed it by a small spring. The pig, scrambling for a hiding place, squeezed itself into a hole in an old tree and waited until it heard dogs barking all around. The bear, fleeing from the hunters, crashed against the tree. Because it was old and rotten, the tree broke in half. Lo and behold, where it broke, it revealed a wild beehive full of honey! The pig loved honey, but it loved the old man more. It ran straight home and dragged him outside again. This time, the old man followed willingly because he trusted the pig's judgment. When he saw all the honey, he hugged and kissed the piglet. He was so happy that God had given him such a good and kind helper for the winter. There was so much honey in the tree that the two of them couldn't eat it all by New Year's Day. They lived from one day to the next like that. The old man allowed the pig to sleep in his bed, and he talked to it like it was a child. They had long and colorful conversations.

The pig could help its owner in the winter when help was needed the most. It would be good to have a pig like that, right?

**Comments**

As cute as it is short, this story is great for children. I suspect that there must have been a third element to it - a third type of food and a third type of danger - but I did not venture to add any. The first two elements demonstrated such practical knowledge about food sources in the winter forest that I was not sure I could match them. The translation was a little challenging for this tale since, as I have mentioned before, the Hungarian language doesn't have gendered pronouns. So instead of deciding whether the pig was a "he" or a "she," I kept it an "it." I leave the decision of pronouns to the next storyteller.

# Part Four

## Anica's Garden of Rarities

*"When Adam and Eve fell from grace, and the angel exiled them from Paradise, Eve felt sorry to leave the beautiful Garden behind. On her way out, she bowed down here and there, pulling up handfuls of flowers; but she couldn't stop, or even slow down, for the angel was following with a flaming sword. When the gates closed behind Adam and Eve and they were left alone in this barren world, Eve planted those flowers to remind people of Paradise."*

(Bukovinian *Székely* folk legend)

Whenever I think of Anna's love for gardens, this simple yet powerful story comes to my mind. You might have noticed that her tales are bursting with flora and fauna. Everything is alive. Carpathian forests expand to the horizon; gardens thrive under caring hands, flowers talk, trees walk, and magic fruit grows heavy in enchanted orchards. People who have a green thumb or an affinity for animals are rewarded with happiness and good fortune. Nature takes care of them in a million ways.

Anna especially liked flowers. She has several stories about them, and I have included the best ones in this chapter. Only one of these six tales (*János of the Bees*) has ever been published before. It seems that editors of previous collections found them too far outside the common structures of traditional folktales—or maybe just glossed over them in search of more heroic plotlines. And yet, where the storyteller's love of nature meets her deep belief in the power of kindness, great stories can sprout even from the most ordinary seed.

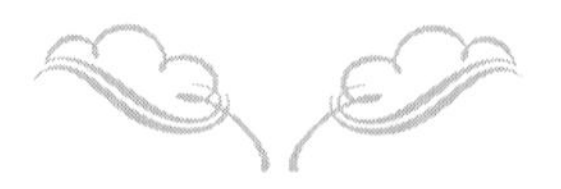

# Mistress Tuberose

I don't even know how to begin this story. It is such a beautiful story that it should only be told with laughter and, right now, I rather feel like crying because my pipe broke. But I will have to tell it anyway, because I know that you girls are curious about how Mistress Tuberose got her name.

Once upon a time, in the middle of a great round forest, there was a large square garden. In the middle of that garden, there was a beautiful castle. Both garden and castle were so splendid that even the sun stopped above them sometimes to admire the view. Birds liked to frequent them—that is, until the Lord of the castle got annoyed by all the singing and chattering and chased them away. I forgot to say that the castle belonged to a great lord (but not a kind one) almost equal in wealth to the King. The Lord had to build an entire village for his servants, drivers and butlers, for there was work for all of them *and* their families in the castle and its gardens.

The Lord had a daughter, a beautiful girl, who loved flowers more than anything. Her father had plants, bulbs, and seeds brought in from faraway countries to make her happy. One day, a package arrived from a Dutch gardener. It was carefully wrapped and labeled, but when they opened it, there were only some scrawny-looking bulbs inside. The Lord grew angry for the bulbs had been quite expensive and did not look promising at all. In fact, he almost threw them out. His daughter begged him to leave them to her and allow a patch for a flowerbed under her window to plant them. She said she could feel that they would grow into something special. While he did not believe she was right, the Lord gave in to his daughter's pleas, but he forbade her from dirtying her own hands with garden work. Instead, he ordered one of the gardeners to do it.

The gardener, not knowing flowers too well, planted the bulbs upside down. Nothing grew from them, even though the girl watched them day in and day out, waiting for a shoot to appear.

Her father grumbled, "The darned Dutchman cheated me! He won't do it again, I swear, because from now on I will only buy what I can see."

But his daughter did not give up so easily. One day, while her father was on a hunt, she snuck into the garden and dug up the bulbs. She saw at first glance that the bulbs were trying to sprout, but they had all been planted upside down, growing down into the dirt instead of up towards the light. She loosened up the soil and re-planted them right side up. After that, she watered them herself every day and watched the tiny green leaves grow happily.

And grow they did—so fast that it was almost visible. One day, stems appeared, shooting up strong and straight. She knew there were going to be flowers at the ends soon because she could see the buds already. She decided not to tell her mother until they had bloomed. Luckily, the summer was not too hot, and the buds unfolded easily. They became beautiful, bone-white flowers, with a scent so sweet and heavy it went straight to your head if you smelled it. It was mostly the girl who smelled them, for no one else knew about the flowerbed. Everyone had long forgotten about the scrawny bulbs.

One day, the gardener walked by and saw the mistress crouching by the flowers and talking to them. *What is she doing?* He wondered. As he stepped closer, and the scent reached his nostrils, he almost keeled over from surprise.

"What gorgeous flowers you have, mistress! Too bad we don't know their name!"

"Don't you remember, Mischa? The bag the bulbs came in said 'tuberose' on it."

The gardener hurried straight to the shed where, among all the springtime odds and ends, he found the discarded bag and the label written by the Dutchman. Now he remembered the scrawny bulbs, too, but he was surprised that they appeared so late. He had planted them in the spring, so why did they only bloom in the summer? He returned to the girl.

"How is it that these flowers are only blooming now?"

"Because the bulbs were planted upside down!" she laughed. "They couldn't grow. I replanted them. But don't tell my father or he'll be terribly angry with both of us. Angry with you for not planting them right and angry with me for getting my hands dirty. But see, wasn't it worth it? They smell so sweet and look so pretty! If I could be this pretty, I would surely marry well."

"You will find a husband, mistress, don't you worry. You are pretty enough," the gardener smiled at her, "even if you are not prettier than these flowers."

As they talked, the lord came home and saw them. He walked up to his daughter and asked what they were discussing so cheerfully. The gardener, being a quick-witted man, came up with an answer first.

"It's just that the mistress would like to be baptized again, sir. She wants to be called Mistress Tuberose."

"What?! You want such a common name for yourself? You could be called Duchess, Golden Flower, Diamond Necklace, or anything noble you wish! Why *tuberose*, out of all things?"

"I will be called Tuberose and nothing else, father, for this flower is so pretty and so sweet, everyone stops to admire it. I think it would make a lovely name."

Blind wrath descended on the lord at hearing that. He thought his daughter was mocking him. He began tearing out the flowers one by one, until only one was left; the girl protected this last stem with her own body. All the screaming and yelling brought the girl's mother outside. Her daughter, with tears in her eyes, begged her mother not to let her father kill her—for if he tore up that last flower, she would surely die with it. This frightened the mother and further angered the father. He was about to drag his daughter away from the flowerbed by force when the gardener stepped in. With his strong hands, he lifted the father, politely yet firmly, and planted him far away from the flowers. The gardener looked his lord straight in the eye.

"I could not make those flowers grow, but the mistress could. She replanted them, cared for them, and that's how the bulbs became flowers. I watched her work in the gardens, with joy on her face, and I would not exchange that for anything, even for a kingdom. If you tear up that flower, I swear I will take it out on you, for I am asking for your daughter's hand in marriage right here and now."

The scent of the flower was not the only thing that made everyone's head reel now. Mischa reached out a calloused hand, and Tuberose slipped her soft fingers into his palm. The two young people stood there, hand in hand, like two children who just found the golden apple of happiness.

The parents stared at each other for a while; finally, it was the father that spoke.

"Listen, son, if my daughter really planted these flowers, that is all well. I'll even let her change her name to Tuberose and allow her to dig in the garden, if she wants to so badly. If somebody does offer you a kingdom, I suggest that you take it because I sure will *not* give her to you as a wife. I have no one else except her and my wife. Go… find yourself a kingdom and leave my daughter alone."

But Tuberose leaned her head on the gardener's shoulder and held on to him so that no one could pry her off. They gazed into each other's eyes and understood each other without words. She finally spoke.

"Dear father, dear mother, we will not go anywhere. All I ask is that you let him keep planting bulbs upside down so I can dig them up, plant them right, and grow such beautiful flowers. For if you don't let me, I will leave with him today. We will cross the Óperenciás Sea, and you will never see me again."

The parents knew their daughter well, and they gave in to her will. Mistress Tuberose became the very happy wife of a gardener who might have been a king—in a different story. They had a great wedding. It was all splendid, but the most beautiful thing was the bouquet of tuberoses that the groom handed to his bride.

Everyone got a tuberose at that wedding. Mine has already wilted. Otherwise I'd show it to you.

**Comments**

The tuberose (*Polyanthes tuberosa*, Hungarian: *tubarózsa, tubavirág*) is a strong-scented flower native to Central America. It crossed the ocean in the 16th century and became a popular garden flower in Hungary by the middle of the 18th century. It even appears in some of our folk songs. It blooms at night, which is why it is also sometimes called Night Queen or Night Hyacinth. Anna doesn't mention the flowers blooming at night. That detail would add a hint of intimacy to the girl's meeting with the gardener and another reason for the father's wrath.

Tuberose blooms mid to late summer, so being planted upside down (while a rookie mistake), was not necessarily the reason for the delay – but shhh, don't tell the gardener. I left these details in because they nicely illustrate how gardeners had to learn by trial and error how to care for freshly imported exotic plants. According to my mother, who shares the gift of the green thumb with this story's protagonist, tuberoses are "terribly fussy" flowers.

In the original text, the gardener suddenly claims to be a prince (instead of saying he would not exchange his joy for a kingdom). I couldn't tell if it was the remainder of some older version of the story where the flowers broke some kind of a curse, or if he meant it metaphorically. In telling the story, I went with the latter. It would also be possible to tell the tale in a way that reveals that he was a prince in disguise and has him giving up an *actual* kingdom for Tuberose in the end. Whatever the reason, I thought it was an interesting hint.

I also left in Anna's endearing introduction before the telling of the tale because it said so much in such few words about both story and storyteller.

Sadly, "Tuberose" is not as alluring a name in English as it sounds in Hungarian (and the mirror translation, "Tubeflower," is not much better either). In fact, when written, it sounds like the mistress has a disease, but I found no way around it. The flower is beautiful with a strong, wonderful scent. And now you have a story for it, too.

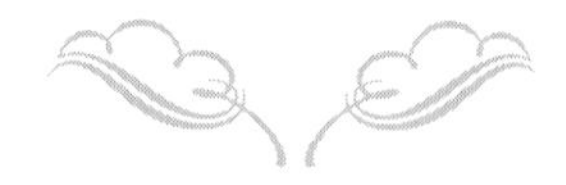

# Touch-Me-Not

This story happened in the old days when everyone still had time to pick flowers in the woods and the meadows.

A little girl was walking in a field one day, picking wildflowers. She tied them into small bouquets so that her mother could sell them to the lords and ladies in the city. It was not a bad way of making money, as the girl could make such expert little bouquets, pretty ones, that even people who did not care for flowers were tempted to buy them. Every morning, on her way to the meadows, the girl stopped at the chapel at the end of the village to pray in front of the statue of the Virgin Mary. She asked the Virgin Mary to give her strength and an abundance of flowers. She always had a spool of yarn with her, spun by her mother during the winter, for tying the bouquets. She also had some bread in her satchel, which was all she would eat until dinnertime. She kept working all day until both baskets on her arms were full.

On this day, as she was picking all the forget-me-nots, pansies, daisies, and cornflowers, she came across a flower she had never seen before. She stepped closer and admired it, but as she reached out, the flower spoke up.

"Little girl, don't pick me! I feel, just like you do. Other flowers feel, too, but they have been created for the joy of people. You can pick them, but please don't pick me. It would bring misery to both you and me."

The girl was surprised by the talking flower, but she did not break it off. She filled her baskets with others and headed home. On her way, she stopped at the chapel again to leave a bouquet for the Virgin Mary. She thought that since she had always been asking, but never giving anything in return, that perhaps the talking flower had been a sign.

The next day she wandered back to the strange little flower again. It was even more beautiful than the day before with its petals shining in the sun. She would have loved to put it into a bouquet, but didn't dare.

The flower spoke again, "Little girl, I know what you are thinking. I know you are tempted, but please don't pick me. Even my name begs you. I am called Touch-me-not."

"How can you talk, if you are a flower?"

"Oh, that is a long story, my dear. If you have time, I am happy to tell you."

The girl sat down in the soft grass ready to listen. Touch-me-not began to speak.

"I used to be a little girl, just like you, before I became a flower. I was not as kind as you are, nor as obedient. I never helped my mother nor did any chores. My mother was not poor like yours, you see, but the greatest lady in the country; she was the Queen. But on the day my little brother Mirkó was born, she died. Soon after, my father married one of the ladies of the court. If anyone can say they have suffered in life, I can. I suffered from the day my father brought his new wife to the castle. In the garden, there was a flowerbed that contained a single flower exactly like I am now. It had been my mother's favorite flower. My stepmother found out, and she ordered the gardener to cut it down. She was Queen now, and she wanted no reminders of her predecessor. In the morning, when my father wanted to pick the flower and take it to my mother's grave, he couldn't find it. He asked the gardener what happened, and, after some hesitation, the gardener admitted that the new Queen ordered it torn up. My father grew angry. He exiled the gardener and told my stepmother that if she did not find a flower just as unique and beautiful by the next day, she would have to leave, too.

She asked for advice in all the wrong places, and some evil people told her what to do. They told her to plant my little brother in the flowerbed, plant him like a seed, and an identical flower would grow. She had a dark enough soul that she did just that; she planted that innocent child, head down, into the ground. I was sleeping when she stole my brother from his bed, and I only woke up when she took him down into the garden. I watched from the window as she planted Mirkó head down and poured a vat of milk on him – the vat was right by the door for she bathed in milk every morning. And lo and behold, there was the same beautiful flower exactly where my brother had been a moment before! The new Queen was happy; she came inside dancing. I was foolish, I began to cry, and yelled at her with threats that I'd tell my father in the morning. I shouldn't have. She grabbed me, snarled at me like a demon, and told me she would tear me apart if I said anything. I continued crying from fright. Then she dragged me here to the meadow and planted me like she did my brother. This is how I became a flower, too. I don't know what happened to my father. Could you go to him, and tell him what I told you? Maybe I could become a girl again, and my father would reward you for your help."

Now that the girl knew the flower's story, she would not have picked it for the world. She caressed it gently and promised that she would go to the King – even if she had to wear her legs down to the knees. The next morning, she told her mother that she would not pick flowers anymore, but instead go far, far away to unveil a great secret. Her mother thought she had lost her mind or maybe gotten a sunstroke. She didn't even force her to go pick flowers that day. She left her at home, telling her to stay in bed and not let anyone in. The girl, however, had already resolved to go. She returned to the flower as soon as her mother was gone and asked for directions to find the King.

"You do not have to go far," said Touch-me-not. "In the closest town that has three churches, that's where my father lives. Tell him to pull up the flower from the flowerbed, careful not to squeeze it, and everything will come to light."

The girl set out. It took her almost a year to find the town with three churches. It wasn't like this in the old days you see. Nowadays, you throw a rock, and you hit a town that has three. But back then, it was rare. When she finally found one, she went straight to the King's castle. There she asked the guards to let her in because she had important things to tell the King.

She was in luck. The King was in desperate need of help, for his new wife was ill. He thought that the girl had brought a cure. But when she entered, the stepmother immediately tried to chase her out; she sensed that trouble had come knocking, and justice would catch up to her. The King didn't let the Queen hurt the little girl, he just ordered that no one should disturb them until she had said all she had to say. The Queen, locked out, began wailing so loudly that the King barely heard what the girl was telling him, but he heard enough. He found out that his children were lost because of their evil stepmother.

"If you can prove this, girl, I will make you a princess!"

"You don't need to make me a princess, Your Majesty. You have a princess of your own. She is still alive, and so is Prince Mirkó. You just need to pull up the flower from the flowerbed, and you'll see."

The King grew angry. Did the girl want him to tear up the most beloved flower of his late wife? It was the only joy he had left in the world. Every once in a while, he would pick some and take them to the first Queen's grave.

"Majesty, if you pull it up so no leaf or root is broken, you will see your son again. I promise."

"Very well then. *You* pull it out, but I warn you. If you are not telling the truth, and my son is not there, I will pull your tongue out like you pull that flower."

The brave girl agreed, and they all went to the garden. The Queen dragged herself out of bed, stumbling three times, and followed them, hoping against all hope that the girl would fail. The King and the entire court watched as the girl embraced the flower as if it was a sick child and pulled it from the ground gently, gently, without breaking a leaf or a root. In that moment, Prince Mirkó stepped out of the flowerbed. He was not little anymore; he was bright and healthy, and he had grown almost to his father's height. The King embraced his son with tears of joy. The Queen would have squeezed herself into any hole to escape, but the courtiers caught her. They wanted to know where the other child was planted. The King, now that he had his son in his arms, wanted to find his daughter, too.

"She is in the meadow where I pick flowers," the girl said. "There is a very beautiful flower in the middle, unlike any other except for the one that had been the Prince. Shall we free her, too?"

"We shall, my little savior," laughed the Prince. But before they could go, they had to see about the fate of the stepmother. The King declared swift justice. A hole was dug by a ditch, and the Queen was planted, head down just like she had done with the children. Believe it or not, she turned into a flower, too, an ugly thorn bush. Everyone that passed by cut her and cursed her.

"That is the punishment for her evil deed," declared the King. He ordered a carriage to be brought about. They all went to the meadow together, making the journey a lot faster than it would have been on foot. And yet, by the time they arrived, the flower was wilting. The girl jumped out of the carriage and ran to her.

"What's wrong, my dear Touch-me-not?"

"I thought you had left me, and I'd never see my father and brother again."

"I didn't leave you! I brought them here to you. See?"

The King recognized his daughter's voice. "My daughter! Oh, how I wish to see her again!"

"You will, Majesty, in a moment. Mirkó, take out your knife and cut down this flower. She is Touch-me-not to everyone else, but she is a sister to you. You can free her."

The King and the Prince hesitated, but they trusted the girl. With a deep breath, Mirkó took out his pocket knife and cut down the flower.

No one who was there ever forgot the tinkling sound it made. Once the tinkling ended, the flower fell, and the Princess stood up, beautiful beyond words. Everyone was happy. They all embraced each other and praised the girl that freed them. Mirkó asked her to marry him straight away.

This is how the flower girl became a queen. Her mother became a royal mother-in-law who cooked, baked, and supervised the royal household. And when the Sun King came to ask Touch-me-not to be his wife, everyone cried so many happy tears that some even fell on the wretched thorn bush. The bush stretched and stretched until it managed to touch her husband's boots. The moment the King stepped on it, the stepmother stood up, now so obedient, and kind, that even the young Queen grew to like her.

Life was happy from that day on. Everyone who saw the royal family envied them for their luck. This is how I heard it, this is how I tell it.

### Comments

The closest parallel to this story is the "Mother Killed Me, Father Ate Me" folktale type (ATU 720) where a child is murdered by its (step) mother, usually by beheading, and then returns in the form of a plant or a bird, bringing the truth to light. Just like in this tale, the victim is often a little boy with an older sister. The most famous example is probably the Grimm's *Juniper Tree,* but the story is widely known in many cultures, including Hungarian and Romanian traditions. Once again, Anna's elegant details transform the story into something unique: the friendship between the girl and the flower, the redemption of the stepmother, and the changing of the abused children into Touch-me-nots are all elements worth paying attention to.

The only "touch-me-not" that is native to Hungary is *Impatiens noli-tangere*, the yellow-flowered wild balsam. While a plant with this name does exist, I was unsure if Pályuk Anna was referring to it specifically or to a magical flower that should not be picked. Whether she got the idea from the name of the real flower, or just happened to use the same term for it, we will never know. If it suits your imagination, picture Princess Touch-me-not with a fragile stalk, elegant leaves, and bright yellow flowers. If some other description strikes your fancy, you can use that too.

Mirkó's name is reminiscent of another, much more famous Hungarian folktale, aptly titled "Prince Mirkó" (*Mirkó királyfi*). The Sun King (*Napkirály*) is mentioned occasionally in stories and attempted reconstructions of Hungarian mythology, although we also have traditions in which the Sun is a woman. In a story in the last chapter, we will encounter this celestial sovereign again.

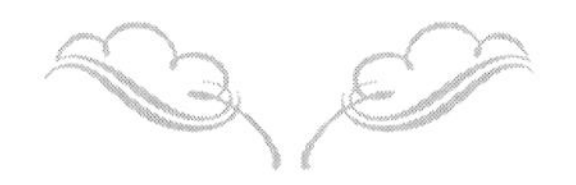

# The King of the Birchwood

I am sure you have heard many stories about all kinds of kings, rich and poor, good and bad, old and young – but I am also sure that no one has told you yet about the King of the Birchwood. I only know this story because my father, when he was serving as a soldier, traveled to a faraway country and heard it there. Since he knew how much we loved stories, he told it to us when he came home. I thought it was beautiful. I am curious to see if you'll like it, too.

Once upon a time, there was a beautiful forest where every tree's bark was so white it was as if it had been freshly painted. Would you like to know why? It happened on the day when the trees decided to elect their own king. They all painted themselves a bright, sparkling white because whoever was deemed the most beautiful was going to rule them all. That was what they decided. The whole forest was made of birch trees, all of them so pretty that it was impossible to pick out the prettiest. The selection lasted a long time. They argued, they debated, and they compared themselves to each other, from root to branch. One was a little crooked, and one was too straight; one didn't have enough branches, and another had too many. The forest was without a king for quite a long time.

The forest also had a forester, like all forests do. One day as he walked around, he saw a birch sapling. He thought it could become a very nice tree as it was just in the right spot to offer shade to travelers. He began to tend to it, straighten it, and prune it. Within a year, the sapling grew into a great big tree with a rich crown that provided cool shade for the forester to escape the noon heat. The forester had to patrol the whole vast forest and make sure people were not stealing wood. He was often tired from walking and, on his way home, enjoyed spending some time under his tree.

One day, as he was resting, the tree suddenly spoke.

"My dear caretaker, my father, would you help me become the King of the Forest?"

*What kind of a miracle is this? A talking tree,* wondered the forester, but the birch had more to say.

"If you could bring some fat to rub into my bark, I would outshine everyone. I would be the most beautiful tree in the forest. The election is tomorrow. We must be quick, and no one can notice."

The forester mused for a little bit, then reached into his bag and pulled out a large piece of bacon. He began rubbing it all over the tree, and lo and behold, the white bark began to shine and gleam. Soon he ran out of bacon; he did not have enough for the whole tree. He ran home for more. He did not even have to go all the way because he ran into his wife on her way home from the market with a fresh chunk of bacon in her basket. The forester took it without a word, returned to his tree and rubbed the bacon fat all over it. Soon this piece ran out, too.

"I can't go home and get more. My wife will be angry at me for wasting all this food," he mused, "but where can I get some more bacon to finish shining up these few branches?"

Then he remembered his friend, the woodcutter that lived on the other side of the forest. He borrowed a piece of bacon from him and finished rubbing the tree. Now the whole tree gleamed and shone. It was a pleasure to look at. It twisted and bowed, admiring itself. Then the tree noted the exhaustion and worry on the forester's face and immediately guessed what ailed him... He had just wasted two weeks' worth of food on a tree, after all.

"I am grateful to you for your help," the birch told the forester. "Come back tomorrow at noon, and I shall reward you."

The forester only half believed the promise. At home, his wife yelled at him for wasting all that bacon. There was nothing to eat, and they went to bed angry and hungry.

Even in bed, the wife kept arguing, "What will we eat this week, or the next? What will I put in the potato soup?"

The forester didn't tell her what happened. He was worried that she would think he had lost his mind. The next day, he only got bread and onions in his bag, and he didn't eat anything until noon when he remembered to go visit his tree.

When he got there, he was surprised to see all the trees bowing, twisting, and gathering around. He barely had space to sit down in the tangle of branches and roots. They were all admiring the shining bark! They all agreed that this birch tree was the most beautiful, the most regal, and the only one fit to be their King. The forester didn't understand the language of the trees, but he did see them place a small golden crown on top of his tree, before they all bowed low. It was enough to tell him what transpired, and he was happy to see his tree become King. Once the celebration was over and the other trees left, the King spoke.

"Dear forester, I shall reward you, not just for the bacon, but also for raising me. From this day on, every day I will grant you as much dry wood as you can carry. You must promise not to take an ax to any tree that is still alive, but you can cut up all the dead ones. There are enough of them to make you rich. And so that no one bothers you about the firewood, here is this document. If you show it, they will let you work in peace. Just keep your promise; you won't regret it."

And so it was. The forester carried enough dry wood home every day that his wife could soon afford to buy bacon, pigs, cows, and everything they needed from the money he earned. They lived comfortably for a while, but eventually, the woodcutter became jealous. He had never been repaid for his bacon, and now the forester was encroaching on his business, too! The woodcutter began spreading rumors in the village that the forester was stealing wood for himself. The poor man was summoned to court.

"What shall we do?" asked the wife.

"Do not worry. I have a document from the King of the Birchwood. I am not afraid."

He took the document and showed it at court, but no one could read it! They thought he was lying or taking them for fools. The judge sentenced him to prison, and his wife waited for him at home in vain.

The King of the Birchwood wondered where the forester had gone. He had gotten used to seeing the hard-working, honest man every day, but now days had passed without him coming to the forest. One day, when an old beggar stopped in his shade to rest, the King spoke.

"Dear old man, I will give you a good sturdy walking staff if you go and find that forester who used to live at the edge of the woods. If you bring news of him, I will reward you." The old man took the staff and set out. He visited the house at the edge of the forest, where the wife sat weeping for her husband. She told the beggar that the forester had been thrown into prison, and she did not even know why.

The beggar continued his journey into town, where he found out that the forester had been imprisoned because he had some document nobody could read about how he was allowed to gather dry wood in the forest. So, the beggar returned to the King of the Birchwood and recounted all he had learned.

"Well, if that is the problem, I will go to the judges and read the document to them," said the tree.

The next day the King set out with seven great birches as his royal guard. Of course, they could not enter the courthouse, but they called the judges outside and ordered them to bring out the document they had confiscated from the forester. The King told them that he had written the document with his own sap on his own bark, and that the forester had broken no law in the Birchwood. The judges were stunned to see a tree talk, and even more stunned to see it come to court to rescue a man.

And succeed.

The document was read aloud for everyone to hear, and the forester was released. After he returned home, he and his wife celebrated for three days in the tree's great shadow, eating and drinking. The King of the Birchwood still remembers that man for his kindness and his loyalty.

I told you that you have heard nothing like this before! But even if it is just a tale, it is good to know that good people are loved even by the trees.

**Comments**

Whenever I dye Easter eggs, I rub a piece of bacon all over them to make the colors shine. As a bonus, it also gives them a delicious scent. Whenever I picture this story in my head, the white birch bark shines in a similar way and smells like breakfast. Hungarian bacon has copious amounts of fat; we often cook it on spits over the campfire and let the fat drip onto a piece of bread. Yum!

Thoughts of food aside, I really treasure the talking-walking birch trees in this story. It is not something that I have encountered in our folktales very often. Birch plays an important part in Hungarian plant lore it is used to ward off curses and enhance fertility. The claim that Anna's father has been to war and brought this story back from some far away country only makes it more interesting. Magical birch trees appear in Slavic tales such as *The Wood Maiden*. There is also a Roma folktale from Transylvania, recently published in a gorgeous picture book that explains why trees don't walk around anymore (*Miért nem tudnak a fák* járni?). If you are having flashbacks to the Ents in *Lord of the Rings*, you are completely right.

I recently found a historical legend from Transcarpathia that combines the love of flowers with plant life going to battle to help a human. According to the story, when Rákóczi (Rákóczi Ferenc II, the famous leader of our 1703-1711 revolution against Habsburg rule) was a child, he protected his mother's prized tulips from a storm. In return, he received a golden trumpet from an angel. When the castle was in danger, the sound of the trumpet turned the tulips into soldiers.

The part about the "document" being written on the King's own bark is my own invention. Writing letters on birch bark was common practice throughout history in the areas where these trees grow in great numbers.

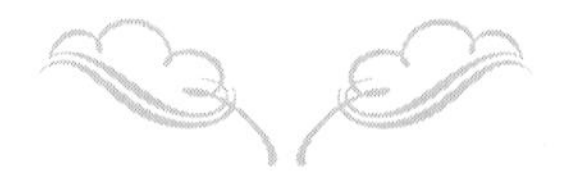

# Little Orphan

Once upon a time, a great tragedy befell a poor woman. Her husband, who was a good man and a hard worker, died. A tree fell on him in the woods. He was brought home and buried. The poor woman sold her last goat to pay for a decent funeral. She had nothing left in the world, but her own two hands and a little, unbaptized girl in the cradle. She had no money left to have her daughter christened in a church, so she did it herself, naming her Árvácska (Little Orphan).

The girl grew like a weed. She needed food; she needed some rags to wear. The mother did what she could to care for her, but Árvácska still went hungry more often than not. The poor woman took in laundry, carried firewood from the forest, and did all the odd jobs a widow could do to earn a few coins.

One day as the mother walked in the woods, she found a small bundle of rags. She took it home and unfolded it, but there were only seeds inside – tiny black seeds. They looked like nothing at all. She didn't trouble herself with them and left the bundle on the table as she went about her chores. But Árvácska, who was six or seven years old at the time, the most curious age, found the rags, took out the seeds, and, since they did not look edible, she decided to plant them in the garden. *Maybe they would bear delicious fruit or some pretty flowers*, she hoped.

By the morning all the flowerbeds were filled with beautiful, colorful flowers, the likes of which no one had ever seen before. Everyone who walked past stopped to peer over the fence and admire the widow's garden. Árvácska spent her day marveling at the flowers, running from one to the other. She didn't know what they were called, and no one else could tell her, so she named them after herself: Árvácska. They were hers, after all.

Things got better from that day on. The mother took the flowers to the city, where rich lords paid well for such novelties. In fact, Árvácska's flowers earned more money than her mother's work ever could. She kept planting the colorful flowers and tending to them, and everyone wanted to buy some. Soon the little family had money to spend.

One day, a splendid carriage pulled up to the house.

"Is this the home of Árvácska, the flower girl?"

"Mine and my mother's," she answered cheerfully. And lo and behold, a real Countess stepped out of the carriage to look the famous flower girl over curiously. She had a little girl with her, four or five years old, and the child ran straight to the flowers, picking her apron full of them. When the Countess saw this, she put an arm around Árvácska's shoulders and asked her to go with them to their castle to make a garden like that. She would be paid well.

Árvácska made a flower garden like no other. In exchange, she was supplied for the entire winter with food, clothes, and anything else she needed. The garden flourished, and the Countess was so satisfied with the arrangement that they repeated it year after year.

One day, the son of the Countess came home from a faraway land and fell in love with the flower girl. When he told his mother that he wanted to marry her, the Countess grew angry – for a count to marry a gardener! But the son retorted that if wealth was more important to her than her own son's happiness, then she could have keep inheritance, and he would go away and marry Árvácska elsewhere. The Countess didn't believe him, but the next week news reached her from the village that the young lovers had wed in secret. When it was all said and done, the Countess forgave them and invited them back. They still live together somewhere, and I am sure they are happy.

These flowers are called árvácska to this very day because the girl was not baptized and grew up wild. But she was also kind, and beautiful much like her flowers. Everyone loves them still.

**Comments**

This entire story hinges on wordplay that is impossible to translate, but it is also too nice to be left out of the book. Pansies in Hungarian are called árvácska (little orphan). They are popular garden flowers and come in many different color combinations. They were cultivated from wildflowers, much like Árvácska herself. I remember being fascinated by them when I was a little girl. My grandmother grew them in flower boxes all around the house, and I spent afternoons trying to copy the colors. Pansies became popular in the 19th century when all the million color variations were created. No wonder Anna loved them, too. She also seems to have had a soft spot for romance involving gardeners and nobility.

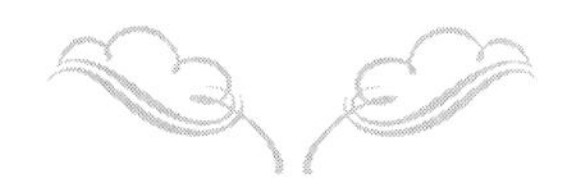

# Szelemen in the Apple Orchard

Once upon a time, a long time ago, so long that there were a lot fewer people in the world than there are now, there was a great war. In that war, many people were captured, and the victor took the captive soldiers away to Saracen land. This is how Szelemen became a prisoner. Szelemen who? I will tell you, but you will have to believe every word I say.

Szelemen's father was a rope maker. He made enough rope in his lifetime that he could have wrapped the world all around with it. When war came, he went to fight together with his son for they loved their King dearly. There was not enough gunpowder and not enough luck. The war was lost, and they were captured along with many others. The father was taken to a great mill where people had to turn the millstones day and night. His son, Szelemen, was taken by a Saracen Lord to guard his apple orchard. You will not believe the kind of apples that grew there! They were the size of cabbages, or even bigger, and they had such a sweet scent it made one's head dizzy. Szelemen was told he could only eat what had fallen from the trees. So, he stood there watching, day after day, waiting for an apple to fall. None did; they all clung to the tree as if they had been glued there. He wished he could taste one, just one – if he was already a prisoner and a servant, he could at least have a sweet apple! But his wish remained a wish.

One day, a great wind started blowing. The trees bowed to the ground, groaning and creaking. Szelemen listened to the trees all night and thought he would surely eat his fill in the morning for, once the storm was over, there would be enough apples on the ground. But alas, as soon as the wind stopped, the Saracen Lord appeared.

"Pick them up, Szelemen, pick all of them up quickly! Whistle while you do it, whistle like a blackbird, for if you go quiet, you will be sorry!"

*I don't care what you say*, thought Szelemen. He picked up the apples, and when he thought he'd picked up enough, he stopped whistling for a moment and quickly took a bite out of one. But he soon regretted it as the apple in his hand began to pull, and it dragged him straight to the Lord. When the Lord saw the servant's mouth full of apple, he grabbed a stick and whacked Szelemen on the head so hard that the apple fell out of his mouth. He began whistling again to avoid being beaten more. The apple had not been that good anyway, it tasted like raw meat. Szelemen never wanted to taste one again.

In the evening, the Saracen Lord went home with all the fallen apples, but the one Szelemen had bit into was left on the ground. Szelemen did not want to eat it, but it looked so alluring that he picked it up absent-mindedly and took it into his cottage. The moment he closed the door, the apple shivered and turned into a beautiful girl right in front of his eyes! Szelemen stared at her, not daring to reach out. He was afraid she was all just an illusion.

The girl spoke softly, "Szelemen, please wrap your blanket around me. I am blue from the cold, see?" she begged, shivering. Szelemen handed her the blanket and was about to leave the cottage, but something held him back. The girl fell asleep in his bed. He sat by the fireplace, guarding her, until he nodded off, too. In his dream he was home, telling people what kind of a garden he had guarded in Saracen lands, with apples large as cabbages and some of them turning into women. No one believed him. They just laughed. He kept repeating his truth, but no one took him seriously. He finally yelled that he would bring an apple to show them. And then he woke up.

The sun was already shining and, where the girl had been, there was only an apple. *I must have dreamed it all*, he thought. *I have been hit on the head too hard*. But in the evening, as the sun set, the apple turned into a girl again, right in front of his eyes. This time he wanted to stay awake, but he couldn't. He had the same dream as the night before. In the morning, the apple was there again, bundled in the blanket, quiet and alluring as ever. Szelemen resolved to run away. If the magic worked the same way at home as it did in the gardens, then he would marry the girl.

In the morning, he said goodbye to the trees. The trees seemed to say goodbye, too, caressing Szelemen with their branches as he passed them. He cut a walking staff from one of the dead trunks, tucked the apple inside his shirt, and set out. He walked all day until he grew tired, and then he lay down to sleep. At night, he felt the weight of someone sleeping on his chest and heard gentle snoring, but he was too afraid to move. By the morning light, the mysterious companion disappeared. This happened every night on the road. On the sixth day, he reached his village.

He was met with a funeral procession. He asked whom they were burying, and found it was his own mother, who had died from grief for her husband and son. He mourned for her, and accompanied her coffin to the cemetery. When she had been laid to rest, Szelemen went home to an empty house. When he took the apple out of his shirt, suddenly bright light filled the room, and there was the girl all dressed in gold, more beautiful than any sight he had ever seen.

Szelemen finally gathered up his courage to speak.

"Who are you, my lady, and where did you come from?"

"You brought me here yourself in your shirt and may God bless you for it. I will send the winds to tell my father to come, and then we will have a wedding, you and I. My father will reward you for saving me from captivity, and we will be happy."

Szelemen escaped one prison, but he fell into another. For the moment he looked into the girl's bright eyes, he was her captive forever, bound and chained with love, and he would not have left her for anything.

In a few hours, a splendid carriage arrived at the house and in it was a white-bearded lord with a large entourage. He hugged his daughter and cried tears of joy. When he found out who rescued her, he happily accepted Szelemen as his son-in-law. He sent messengers with gold to Saracen land immediately to ransom Szelemen's father from captivity. Once the father returned and regained his health, they held a great wedding with all kinds of food – even apples (but the real kind, not the kind that tastes like flesh). After the wedding was over and the guests left, the young couple lived on in love that grew brighter day by day. Maybe they still live together today.

**Comments**

Once again, we have people turned into trees (allegedly), apples behaving badly, and a beautiful maiden rescued by a loyal hero. Apple maidens are common in Western folklore; they usually come in threes and belong to the "Three Oranges" folktale type (ATU 408). The most commonly known version, Giambattista Basile's *The Love for Three Oranges*, features fairy maidens born from oranges (or citrons), but around Europe several other fruits are featured, too, from figs to apples (or, in some Hungarian folktales, reeds, and oak branches). The fruit usually has to be sliced open to reveal the maiden, who immediately asks for water. If she is not given any, she dies from thirst. In this story, Szelemen marks the apple by biting into it. I wonder if some earlier telling might have included a wound or a bite mark on the maiden, or had something to do with why she had to sleep for three nights in a row.

The father's ransom from the mill at the end is my addition to the story. Since we learned so much about him at the beginning of the tale, I felt like his story deserved some closure as well. Anna loved joyful, happy endings, and so do I.

There is a play on words in this story, too, that was impossible to translate. When Szelemen is told to whistle, "I don't care what you say" is my translation for *fütyülök rád*, which literally translates into "I whistle at you," and it means the same. Szelemen is not actually a Hungarian name; it literally means ridge-pole, the part of a house. There is another name, Kelemen (Clemens) that sounds very similar except for the first letter. It is possible that Anna mispronounced it, the collector misheard it, or that the storyteller simply made the word into a name for fun. Maybe it will catch on with this story. It certainly has a ring to it.

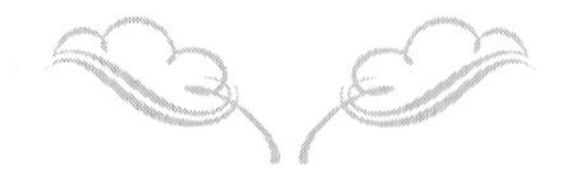

# János of the Bees

Once upon a time, there was a poor man who had a son. The boy might have been a little simple, but he worked hard. He began working at the age of ten, and he made enough money so that his father and mother did not have to pay for his keep. He went to town every day looking for odd jobs to do. If there was some task that required hard work, people always called on him because he was not picky and did not ask for much. He always thanked them politely for the payment and, if they underpaid him a little, he never thought to complain. With this reputation, the boy named János always found work.

Apart from his strength, he also had another talent. He could mimic the buzzing of bees with his mouth. Every time a swarm escaped, János was called to lure the bees back into their hive. János would stand under the tree where the swarm was and buzz and hum until all the bees flew to his hands. None of the bees ever stung him. Sometimes he went out to the meadows and came home with a pretty swarm of wild bees perched on his hat. Those wild hives were good luck, and they sold for good money. Everyone called him Dongó János, János of the Bees.

One day, he was walking home merrily buzzing along with a hive on his head when a good-for-nothing lad saw him and thought it would be amusing to hit János on the hat with a rock to stir the bees. But the lad soon regretted this idea because the moment the rock hit the hive, the bees all swarmed straight after him and stung the lad all over until he died a painful death. News of the incident spread like wildfire, and people began treating János with a lot of respect. When they saw him walking with a swarm, they gave him a wide berth so that they would not end up like that one foolish lad.

One day, János was in the forest with his father cutting wood. Looking up, they saw a great black cloud.

"This looks like a storm," the father said. "We should head home."

"Don't worry father, that's not a cloud. It is a swarm, larger than I have ever seen. Let's catch them!"

János reclined on a little hill and began to hum and buzz. The cloud lowered itself to the sound. At a closer glance, it became clear these were not bees, they were wasps! János knew that this many of them could kill a horse with their stings. He stopped buzzing and began to whistle, as he jumped up and ran down the hill. All the wasps settled where he had been a moment before.

Now that the wasps had settled, they had to be killed because wasps kill off regular bees, and the hives of the village needed to be protected. János and his father went into a nearby house, boiled some water, carried it to the hill, and splashed it all over the wasps. The ones that did not die immediately swarmed up, and even a half-dead wasp can sting like no other. János was nimble and avoided them all, but his father was not so lucky. He got stung twice. He grew so angry at his son that he chased János away from home.

János wandered around the woods for days. He ate strawberries and blackberries, but he was hungry for real food. In a nearby village, he found a farmer who hired him as a swineherd. He had to take the pigs out to the pasture in the morning and bring them back at night; it was not complicated work.

This went well for a week or two. One day János met a wandering student who told him they should go work for the King because he paid his servants better. János suspected that his wages were low, since he could barely afford food and clothes, but it was not in his nature to complain. The wanderer convinced him that they could make their fortune in the royal court. So, János agreed to go.

As they walked along the road, they came across a swarm of bees. János stopped immediately, out of habit, and began to hum and buzz. The bees settled on his hat. The other boy stared at him in awe.

"Why on earth do you work as a swineherd if you can do something like *that*? You can catch as many bees as you want, have many hives, make honey, and *we* could live like lords!"

They began gathering swarms straight away, but both lads forgot that bees needed a hive; there would be no honey without it. János had already gathered five or six swarms. He was down to his pants for he had put his coat, his vest, and then his shirt on top of his head for the bees to gather upon.

"You can't appear in public like this," the student said. He went into town himself, sold the six swarms at a high price, and promised to deliver them personally to those who paid. He got six coins for each swarm, and then he told people that if they needed more, he could take orders. Farmers who had hives ready were happy to fill them, and they began to produce honey.

While the boy was busy selling the swarms, János was standing there on the road half naked. As night fell, János was cold and beginning to wonder if his friend would ever return with his clothes. As the hours passed, it seemed less and less likely. Looking around for shelter, János saw light, and the light led him to a house surrounded by beehives, so many he couldn't even count them.

*This will be a good place for me. I can bring bees here*, he said to himself, and then knocked on the door. A kind-looking old man opened it.

"Good evening to you!"

"And a good evening to you too, my son!"

*This will be a good place for me*, János thought again. The old man saw he was only wearing pants and felt pity for him.

"Where are your clothes? Have you been robbed?

"I have, and badly. I will tell you how. I am called Dongó János. They named me after my talent. I can hum and buzz, and bees that are near me come and sit on my head, my hands or whatever I give them. Yesterday, when I did that, a student, with whom I was planning to be a swineherd for the King's court told me to put all my clothes on my head to catch many bees and get many hives. He said that we would be rich. So, I gave him all my clothes with the swarms, and I think he ran away with them. He must have sold them. I felt cold, and I saw your house, so I came here."

"It is good that you did, son. One of my swarms escaped yesterday. If you have this talent, you may be able to help me get more bees. I never took anything that belonged to others, unless they took something of mine, and I got all that I have by the grace of God. He must have sent you to help me. I can't pay you, but if you work with me, I will share the hives with you."

János agreed. The old man gave him dinner and clothes (not new ones, but at least decent ones). The next morning, they went out together. The old man, as kind as he was, wanted to see with his own eyes what the boy could do. Anyone could say they had a talent, after all, but it had to be proven, too. As noon approached, the bees began to buzz in the meadow.

"Show me, János of the Bees, that you have earned your name!"

"Master, give me the hive you want them to go into. I will call them in."

"Leave it, János, they won't stay. They are all a-buzz," the old man said skeptically, and didn't even want to bring out the hives.

But János noticed the hives nearby. He quickly put one on his head, held one in each hand, and one between his legs, and he began to buzz and hum. And to the old man's astonishment, the moment the bees heard him, they all gathered into the hives. He almost cried tears of joy as he saw his bees return.

"Son, no one will inherit these hives after my death, but you. Just take good care of them."

They soon began supplying all the nearby towns with the sweetest honey anyone had ever tasted. János gathered so many bees that they barely knew where to put them. Soon, they began building multi-story hives. Their honey was so rich and golden that when the King stopped by on a hunt, he got a taste for it, too. János became the wealthiest man in the land. He sent a man to visit his old parents. When they were found living in deep poverty, János went himself to fetch them in a carriage. He nursed them back to health with his best honey. They moved into the house and learned to help with the hives. János got married and continued working all his life by catching bees with his humming. To the end of his days, he was known as Dongó János, even though his sons went by different names.

**Comments**

Here is another unique tale, one that I hope will bring much joy to storytellers who are passionate about bees and beekeeping. I only evened it out a little, where János' own account of how he had been robbed did not match with what happened earlier in the story. Since his monologue made more sense, I adjusted the previous events accordingly.

János is a unique character; he is a "simple-minded" young man with an extraordinary talent. Some people are annoyed by him or afraid of him, some try to take advantage of him, and some kind souls see not just his potential, but also his good heart. The old man who does, helps János find his place in the world and make his own fortune. Famous Hungarian writer Móra Ferenc notes a folk saying from the plains: individuals with mental disabilities were called *többel jó*, which literally translates into "good while with others." As long as others were around, treating them well and helping them along, they were functioning members of society just like anybody else.

*Dongó* in Hungarian can mean either of two things, "bumblebee" (as a noun), or "humming/buzzing" (as an adjective). I translated it as "János of the Bees," but it could just as easily mean "Humming János" or

"Buzzing János." We also have different words for a hive of bees (*méhraj*) and the hive bees live in (*méhkas*). Where both were mentioned in the story next to each other, I used "swarm" and "hive" to make things easier to differentiate.

# Part Five

## Love in All its Strangeness and Glory

This final chapter contains some of Pályuk Anna's most magical tales. They all have something to do with love, but they are also alike in the incredible richness of the imagery they contain. These are the long tales where Anna let her imagination and her creativity run wild. She takes us from enchanted fields of lilies-of-the-valley all the way to the "Cloud Kingdom." One story links into the next, giving a hint that they might have, in her mind, all taken place in the same world of magic and adventure. These were the stories that first piqued my interest in their storyteller and the ones I have told most often on stage. They always inspire curiosity, laughter, and awe from their audiences. Treat them with care and respect. They are all one of a kind.

# The Dream of the Fairy Queen

Once upon a time, I don't know where or how far away—only my father knew for he has been to war and seen many things—there was a very, very rich man. This rich man had a son whose name was Jakab. Jakab was a handsome young man, and he could have gotten a handsome name too. But instead, of all things, they named him *Jakab*. Other boys mercilessly mocked him for it all his life. He was sad about having such a strange name, and he finally told his parents that since they could not name him right, he would leave and seek his fortune elsewhere. His parents cried, not knowing if they would ever hear from him again. Jakab ignored their tears and left in a flurry of youthful indignation.

He walked and walked until he arrived at a great forest. Night was falling, and he began looking around for a place to sleep. As he searched, he noticed something vastly out of place: A neat little carriage, barely bigger than a child's toy, drawn by four white swans. As he walked closer, he was even more stunned to see a tiny man, no larger than his thumb, inside the carriage. Jakab had never seen, or even heard of, such a creature before. The little man suddenly sneezed and sat up. The sneeze startled Jakab so much that he stumbled and sat down hard. The little man laughed a tinkling laugh and kept laughing even harder when he saw Jakab's confused expression.

This little man was no other than the Seneschal of the Court of Tündér Ilona, Queen of the Fairies. He told Jakab that he had come to the forest to see if the lilies-of-the-valley were blooming yet, so that the Queen could come with her maids and make bouquets.

"Lilies-of-the-valley? I can show you a place where they grow so thick that the Queen can pick an armful sitting down!" Jakab said.

"I will tell her that, and if it is so, you will be rewarded," the little man promised.

"Even if I am not, I will still be happy to show you. It is the most beautiful forest of lilies-of-the-valley I have ever seen."

Jakab barely finished his sentence when music drifted through the woods, and Tündér Ilona appeared with her entire court. The young man's eyes grew wide, for he had never seen anything quite so beautiful in his life as the Fairy Queen and her ladies. Not even a host of angels could have been a more amazing sight.

"Is it true that you can lead us to a forest of lilies-of-the-valley?"

"It is true, Tündér Ilona, Your Majesty."

Jakab turned and waved to them to follow. He led the fairies to a part of the forest where the ground was covered in white, pearl-like flowers. But what he didn't realize was that the grove was also cursed. Whoever entered it would immediately turn into something else. The moment they walked in, he saw one fairy maiden turn into a frog, another into a lizard, and a third into a blackthorn bush. Jakab himself turned into an old man holding a large shepherd's staff.

"I just *had* to make a promise to the fairies, didn't I?" he muttered bitterly.

Tündér Ilona felt pity for the young man, for she had taken a liking to him. She promised that she would get her brother, who was Lord of the Forest, to free him right away. But fairies are fickle and, as soon as she returned home, she got distracted by something shiny and forgot all about Jakab.

Time passed.

One night the Fairy Queen saw a dream. In her dream, she was reminded of the maidens and the mortal that were left out in the forest, although she didn't quite remember who the mortal was. The dream also told her that she needed to save him from the spell, or he would be lost, and Fairyland would be lost with him.

In the morning, she went to her brother.

"I had such a strange dream. Give me advice, please! What should I do?

The Lord of the Forests listened to her story, and asked her, "What do you want to do with that Jakab lad?"

Ilona shivered at the terrible name, but she also remembered the face of the young mortal. She decided she could learn to live with the name, if she could live with him.

"I would prefer that he was called something else, but he is not. And I would never leave his side, whatever he is called."

"Very well. But to save him, the Forest Spirit has to be defeated."

Ilona grew sad. How could her handsome mortal defeat the Forest Spirit? Still, she went to the forest the next morning and looked for the old man. She searched for a long time, but couldn't find him. She finally grew hungry and was about to pick some strawberries when the old man appeared, shepherd's staff raised to whack her on the hand. He was guarding the forest and everything in it.

"You are a loyal man, Jakab," Ilona smiled at him.

"How do you know that ugly name? I thought I would never hear it again. I hated it so much I left my mother and father because of it. Now I wish I never did. My name is still with me, I could not leave it behind. And maybe grief has already killed my parents since I left."

Tündér Ilona felt pity for the mortal. He had such a kind heart; he deserved her help. But how? She thought about it so long she became sleepy again. She was not used to thinking about only one thing for this long, you see. She lay down to take a nap. The old man gently put a bundle of fern leaves under her head as a pillow and guarded her sleep, his heart aching. She was a fairy queen, and he was just an old man who would never be young again.

Meanwhile, Tündér Ilona had another dream. In her dream, she learned that the fern had given her power to defeat the Forest Spirit. As soon as she heard this, she woke up, smoothed down her skirts, rubbed her eyes, and called out.

"Come out, Forest Spirit, and fight me for Jakab!"

Jakab was stunned. This beautiful lady wanted to fight *for* him? He could not believe his luck. As he stared at her, the Forest Spirit appeared in a puff of smoke. How could she defeat *that*? Jakab quickly handed his staff to Ilona, so that she would at least have a weapon. To his astonishment, the Fairy Queen beat the Forest Spirit so soundly, it could barely twitch in the end. Before it perished, however, the Spirit whispered its last words to Jakab.

"If she had not killed me, you would have wasted away within a month. She loves you, and there is no need for me anymore. But be careful! Fairies are fickle; there might come a time when she forgets you again."

The Forest Spirit said all this, and meant it, too. It had always known Ilona to be fickle. But this time, the Forest Spirit was wrong about her. The moment it died, Jakab turned into a young man again, and Tündér Ilona offered him her hand.

"Jakab, I will not go back home until we have your parents' blessing to marry."

"Well then, my flower, let us go home."

They set out together, hand in hand; but neither of them realized that a lot of time had passed between Jakab turning into an old man and turning young again. By the time they arrived at his home village, only his mother was still alive. She was so old she couldn't see. She stumbled around blindly grasping at things. When the handsome young man and the beautiful woman came to ask for her blessing, she began to cry. She had long forgotten that she ever had a son called Jakab.

"Mortals have short memories," said Tündér Ilona sadly. "The woman who gave birth to you forgot all about you. If she forgot, everyone else must have forgotten, too. From now on, you will not be called Jakab. I will call you Párom. My Love."

"I like that," he answered with a smile. There was nothing in the village for him anymore, but he wanted to go to the old church to pray one more time before they left. As they walked down the street, an old woman stepped in front of them.

"Jakab, your mother and father cried many tears because of you. You father died, your mother lost her mind. But happiness can still cure her. Where have you been all this time? We all thought you got lost in the woods like the priests' donkey!"

"If you remember me, Auntie, why does my mother not know me?"

"There is a way to remind her. But don't tell anyone I told you. Go to the graveyard, and next to your father's grave there is an open pit. Stand in it, and yell 'If I owe you something, come here, and I will settle the debt!' There will be much commotion, but do not be afraid. Just hold this holy candle over your head, and everything will turn out well."

Once the old woman walked away, the young man turned to his bride.

"Will you come with me, Ilona?"

"I will wait for you in the churchyard and rest."

Tündér Ilona first lay down in a flowerbed, but she soon grew bored and wandered into the church. She poked around curiously, tiptoeing between the pews and marveling at the crosses. She finally found a silver incense burner hanging on its chains and thought it was pretty. She unhooked it and walked around, giggling as wisps of scented smoke began to waft from it. She finally lay down in a pew and fell asleep.

Meanwhile, the young man went to the graveyard, stood in the pit, and called out, "If I owe you a debt, come, and I will settle it!"

Lo and behold, all the demons, ghosts, devils, and lost souls that were in the world began to swarm around the pit, trying to devour him. The flame of the holy candle flickered dangerously. Tündér Ilona, who dreamed that her love was in danger, jumped up and ran to stand by his side. As she ran, the incense burner she was still holding swung around, spreading smoke everywhere. The holy scent chased all the evil creatures away from the strongest demon to the last limping devil. The lovers were free.

By the time they got home, Jakab's mother was cheerfully cooking dinner. She embraced her son in tears and laughter, and she also hugged her new daughter-in-law, Ilona. For in the graveyard, the Queen had lost her fairy nature, and now she was mortal, too – not a *Tündér* anymore. But she was happy.

Jakab and Ilona got married, and now they have a beautiful family like no other in the village. Ilona milks the cows, washes the linen, and works like any other woman, only with more grace. Her mother-in-law lives with them, raising all the little Jakabs and Ilonas, and tells them the tale of the Dream of the Fairy Queen. It was a good dream; my grandfather used to say we all need more of those. Jakab is not even angry about his name anymore.

This is the end of the story. Take it, and give it to someone else.

## Comments

Jakab (Jacob), while not a very common name in Hungary, is not weird enough to merit all the conflict in this story. I can't quite tell if in Anna's time it was rarer, or she just personally thought it was funny, or it was considered "strange" because it is a name of Jewish origin. It certainly adds some difficulty to this tale—if one picks another name, any name, to make fun of, it is guaranteed that there will be at least one person in the audience who is called just that (as a person with a rare name, I can relate). Sometimes I tell this story, and I don't tell the audience what the hero was called; I simply state that he had a weird name, so weird indeed that I'd rather not say it out loud. Everyone can make up their own mind.

*Párom* literally means "my partner" or my "my pair." It is a gender-neutral term still used for one's significant other.

Tündér Ilona is a very popular figure in Hungarian folklore. *Tündér* means fairy; she is also sometimes called *Tündérszép Ilona,* "Ilona beautiful as a fairy." She is often the maiden to be rescued or the bride to be returned in our folktales – although she can have a mean streak when she is angered (or if somebody is prettier than her). She is usually human-sized, only more beautiful, which is important to note since her Seneschal appears in this story as a tiny figure. Hungarian fairies are usually human-sized, and, not unlike the Elves in Tolkien's *Lord of the Rings*, they have their own castles, powers, and social hierarchy. Tündér Ilona rules over Fairyland, but I have never encountered another story in which she has a brother who is the Lord of the Forest. Given that the forest plays such a central part in all of Anna's stories, it is no wonder that it appears in this tale twice, both as a caring brother and as an antagonist. Furicz János also had a tale about the Forest Spirit, in which the Spirit helps a forester protect the trees from woodcutters. The belief that the fern (or the fern's elusive flower) has magical properties is common both in Hungarian and wider European folklore.

I added a small scene to this story, the one where Ilona wanders into the church. In the original text, she falls asleep in the flowerbed, sees a dream, wakes up, and runs straight to the cemetery with an incense burner in hand. Since we have already learned that she is fickle and curious, I imagined she would have come across it by investigating a building she has never seen before. When I tell the story, I sometimes also add a moment where Jakab uses the flickering holy candle to re-ignite the incense burner; that way, they defeat the demons together. If you like it, you can add it, too.

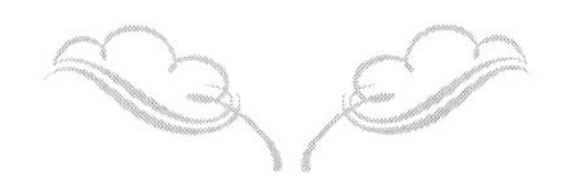

# The Boy Who Wanted to Walk on the Clouds

Once upon a time, there was a widow. All she had in the world was her son and a little cow. She worked day and night for both. She took the cow to pasture every day, and dressed and fed her son as if he were the heir of a nobleman. He never had to work a day in his life. He spent all his time lying around in the soft green grass, looking up at the clouds, dreaming about what it would be like to walk on them. They looked so pure, so white, and so *soft*, from down below. He longed to fly up and touch them.

Time passed, and one day the old woman died, leaving her son alone with the cow. The boy didn't know what to do. He had no practice with running a household, and he barely knew how to care for livestock. He decided it was time to make his dreams come true. He would give the cow to whoever could tell him how to reach the clouds.

There was a woodcarver who lived at the end of the street. People regarded him as the wisest man in the village. The boy went to him, leading the cow.

"Good day to you, son," the woodcarver greeted him. "Are you looking to be an apprentice?"

"No, Uncle. I am looking to find out how I can reach the clouds. If you can tell me, I will give you this little cow. I can't take it with me on such a long journey anyway."

*Well, well*, the woodcarver thought to himself, *if I don't tell this silly boy something, he will just find someone else who will lie to him. I might as well get the cow for myself, if it comes so cheap*. So, he lied. He told the boy what he wanted to hear, and took the cow happily home. The little cow ate its fill on the new pasture and gave two full buckets of milk that night.

"Where did you get such a nice cow? I hope it wasn't too costly?" asked his wife, and the woodcarver gave her a cheerful wink.

"All I had to do was tell the simpleton how to get to the clouds!"

The wife furrowed her brow.

"You cheated that poor orphan boy out of his cow? Are you not afraid that God will punish you?"

"Why would He? I told the boy what he wanted to hear. He would have given that cow away sooner or later anyway. You know him, he would have never known what to do with it! And if he sets out to seek his fortune, he might even find it along the way."

That was that, between the woodcarver and his wife. As for the boy, these are the instructions he received in exchange for his cow:

"See that mountain far to our left? Walk all the way there, go up the mountain, and you will find a little house. From the roof of the house, you can easily step onto the clouds, and walk all over them as long as you want."

The boy set out towards the mountain. He traveled for a long time with only a satchel of food, but his goal barely seemed to get any closer. He stopped for the night in the woods, ate a few bites, and found a spring from which to drink. As he leaned over the water, something caught his eye. A beautiful little weasel was trapped in the bushes, desperately squirming around.

"Oh, poor little one," the boy muttered, carefully freeing the weasel from the thicket.

The tiny creature thanked him for his help, and gave him a single hair from her soft fur, saying, "If you ever needed help, take the hair out and call out to me!"

The boy chuckled as the weasel disappeared in the woods. Why would he ever need help from such a tiny creature? But he put the hair away anyhow and lay down to sleep.

When he woke the next morning, he felt tired and sad. He was far from home, alone. As he opened his eyes, the sunlight dancing in the trees seemed to be laughing at him, mocking his dream to walk on the clouds.

A blackbird nearby seemed to be saying "Foolish boy, silly boy!"

The boy grew angry and chased the bird, further and further through the woods. He chased it all day, until night was about to fall. Looking up, he realized he was at the foot of the mountain.

*I'll climb up and find that little house tomorrow*, he told himself, and settled down to sleep. Suddenly, something tugged on his sleeve. Looking down, he noticed the weasel at his elbow.

"I have found a job for you!" she chirped. "The King of the Mountains is about to go on a journey to see the world. He is looking for someone to accompany him. He will travel through the air and never touch the ground. It is not quite the clouds, but it is one step closer! I already recommended you as a companion. Come along, hurry, he is about to leave! They are waiting for you."

The boy jumped up instantly and ran up the mountain, following the weasel. By the time the sun was rising, he had made it to the very top. He found no little house there, but there was a splendid carriage drawn by two fiery horses. Inside the carriage sat a King, as old and wrinkled as the mountainside itself. He was dozing.

The weasel tumbled and turned into a carriage driver, taking her seat and gathering up the reins.

"Take your seat inside," she told the boy. "If you feel sick as we take off, close your eyes. Once we are up in the air, you can look around. You will see many things no mortal has ever seen before. But remember my words: *never* show that you are surprised or afraid. Pretend you have seen it all before."

The boy knew he could trust the weasel's advice. He got into the carriage and closed his eyes. Off they went, flying through the air, and the whole world seemed to be spinning around him.

"You can look now!" the driver called out. The boy opened his eyes and looked out the window, admiring the landscape far below: Rivers looked like ribbons, houses looked like toys, and fields like a patchwork quilt.

Suddenly, the view was obscured by something. An eye, as large as the window, peered inside the carriage. The King woke with a start and cried out, clinging to the boy in fright, "A giant! A giant!"

"It is all well, Your Majesty," the boy smiled, showing no fear. "No reason to be afraid of a puny thing like that."

The King, seeing the boy was not scared at all, relaxed his grip. The giant stooped away from the carriage, leaning down to continue his work of hoeing the long rows of his vineyard.

"Look!" pointed the King "Those grapes are each larger than a table!"

"Oh well," the boy shrugged. "I have seen grapes seven times larger than these, Your Majesty!" The King looked at the boy, clearly impressed. On and on they traveled across the skies and saw many wonders: palaces hanging in the air by golden threads, firebirds soaring high above, even a dragon's serpentine tail disappearing into a storm cloud. The boy drank in all that he could see, but never showed surprise or fear.

Finally, they arrived at a field of clouds. They looked like a flock of sheep, dyed pink and gold by the setting sun. The boy couldn't wait any longer. He tore open the door of the carriage and stepped out onto the nearest cloud.

The carriage instantly disappeared. The boy was all alone. He stood, basking in the light of the setting sun, enjoying the sensation of standing on a cloud, savoring the knowledge that his dream had finally come true. When the silence grew long, he pulled out the hair of the little weasel, and she immediately appeared at his feet.

"What is your wish?"

"I wish there was a way to let people know that I am up here. That I made it all the way to the clouds" the boy said.

"Is that all? Put your hand here on this cloud. I will put this piece of glass under it; it is attached to one corner of the world. If you push down on it, the earth will tilt and shake, and everyone will see that it is you who has the power do such a thing."

The boy shook his head.

"I don't want that. I don't want to hurt anyone. I just wish the man who thought I was a simpleton would know that I am here. I know he never thought I would make it."

"That is easy," the weasel led the boy across the clouds and stopped at a certain place. "His house is directly below us. If you drop your hat, it will fall right down on it, though I am afraid the house itself might collapse."

How could a hat make a house collapse? The boy laughed at the notion. He took off his hat and dropped it; the hat fell, fell, fell straight down… and when it hit the roof of the woodcarver's house, it broke straight through. The house fell apart like a pile of toothpicks. The woodcarver and his wife, as well as the rest of the village, all ran up to the ruins and found the hat perched on top.

"Isn't that the hat of that silly lad that wanted to walk on the clouds?"

They all looked up as one; and far above, dangling his legs over the edge of a fluffy cloud, the boy waved at them with a wide, bright smile.

He has never been seen since.

**Comments**

Or has he? I like to think that this story and the next one (*The Daughter of the Táltos King*) are closely connected. In my storytelling mind, the silly boy and the Cloud King are one and the same.

I have already mentioned that the Hungarian language does not have gendered pronouns. The original text doesn't say if the weasel is male or female. Calling her a "she" is my personal choice. I also added the part about castles, firebirds, and dragons; the original story only includes the giant and his vineyard. In imagining what else one would see on a flying chariot ride across the skies of Hungarian folklore, I added elements from other tales (or, in the case of the storm dragon, from folk belief). Pretty much everything else in the story follows the original text.

Once again, this story is unique, as it doesn't fall into any established folktale type. Pályuk Anna seems to be weaving motifs of folklore into a new tale through her own creativity. The King of the Mountain appears in other Hungarian tales; the weasel is a rare creature to find in folklore, but does tie into some old Hungarian historical legends. In the 10th century, we had a very feisty queen consort, the mother of our first Christian king, who was called Sarolt, "white weasel."

I like this folktale for its many implications about the way one can achieve their dreams, despite mockery or discouragement, and no matter how silly they sound. It is also a great story to muse about if you (like me) have flight anxiety. I like it for its charm and clarity, and most of all, I like it for the imagery. I have told it many times, and it is always a pleasure to tell.

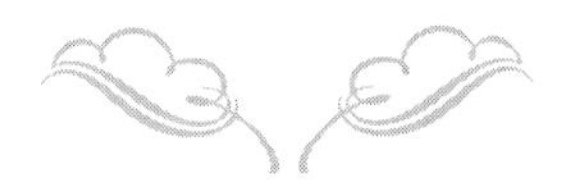

# The Daughter of the *Táltos* King

Once upon a time, on the shores of the bottomless sea, there was a castle and in that castle lived the *Táltos* King. He had such power that he could dry out the sea at will or crumble mountains into dust. He used his power frequently, and people feared him for it. And yet, he was not happy. There was only one thing in the world his powers could not do: they could not cure his only daughter.

The *Táltos* Princess was beautiful, but she only had one leg and one hand. This bothered the King for he believed that no one would ever want to marry her. Many people came to court her, but when they saw that she was missing limbs, they left, one after another. This made the King sad. Power and wealth were useless if there was no one to whom he could leave his kingdom.

One day his daughter said to him, "Dear father, do not worry about me. There is still a way to make sure someone will rule the kingdom after you."

"How can that be, dear daughter?"

"My nurse told me that there is a magic fish in the sea, a fish that appears only once a year, and each time, fulfills one wish."

The King summoned the nurse immediately, and she confirmed what she had told the Princess. She added that the fish would only appear to those whose hands were clean of blood, and that she did not know the day it would come. The King immediately went down to the seashore and waited, waited. He had been waiting almost a whole year, sleeping on the sand and eating food his servants carried down from the castle, but the fish still had not appeared.

One morning, as he sat there, he heard a scream. Turning around, he saw his daughter being carried away from the castle by a strange man. Forgetting about the fish, he hurried to her rescue, drew his sword, and killed the kidnapper. In that very moment, the fish appeared from the sea and turned into a man. The King ran to him, asking for a hand and a leg for his daughter so that she could be happy.

"I only fulfill the wishes of those whose hands are clean of blood," the fish said, "Yours are still dripping with the blood of the man you killed."

"How do you know?"

"I know because he was my brother. He was cursed, and his curse could only be broken if he married a princess with only one leg. But that does not matter anymore. You have lost your right to a wish."

With that, the fish returned to the bottomless sea.

The King regretted now that he'd killed the kidnapper, but there was no turning back. He had to go home and live like he had before. They held balls and feasts and banquets, but no one appeared who would marry the Princess. The King worried himself sick that the kingdom would die with him.

One day a strange sound was heard from above. A basket descended from the sky, suspended from an iridescent cloud. In the basket sat a handsome young man. Once he landed in the palace gardens, he stepped out and looked around curiously. The Princess was sitting by the flowerbeds, propped upon pillows and marveling at the strange sight. The moment the curious visitor locked eyes with her, his face lit up with admiration. He begged her to marry him and go with him to his kingdom that was beyond the clouds. He was none other than the King of the Clouds himself.

"How could I go anywhere?" the Princess asked, although she took an immediate liking to the strange traveler. "Can't you see I am missing a foot and a hand? I can't even walk to the gardens by myself. No one ever proposed to marry me."

"I do not ask you to walk anywhere." The young man smiled, taking her by her one hand, and helping her into the basket. The next moment, they rose into the clouds.

The young King navigated the basket over the kingdom, so the Princess could see the land and its people from above. Floating like a cloud, she saw the rivers like ribbons and the woods like lush tapestries. She could see flocks of birds and the occasional dragon or two. The King of the Clouds showed her his fields, his mountains, and his palaces all built from the same soft, white material.

By the time they landed in the evening, back at the Princess's garden, she had agreed to marry him.

The *Táltos* King, however, did not want to let his daughter go. He was glad to finally find a son-in-law (and royalty, too!), but he demanded that the young man should stay with them, on the ground, and not take the Princess away from home. He refused to give his blessing otherwise. The King of the Clouds insisted that there would be trouble if he stayed away from his own realm. But the Princess looked at him so sweetly, so nicely, that in the end, he agreed to stay.

Days passed. Years passed. The young Queen now had a baby boy. But the kingdom suffered, for there was no rain. While the King of the Clouds was away from his kingdom, drought swept across the land. Something had to be done. The *Táltos* King watched his people, poor and rich alike, suffer from thirst. In the end, he summoned the old nurse again for advice. Her answer was easy, although not the one he'd hoped to hear.

"Let your daughter go with her husband, and we will have rain."

The *Táltos* King could not find it in his heart to let his only daughter go. He loved her, and loved his little grandson more than anything. Finally, as a compromise, the young royal couple agreed to leave the little Cloud Prince in his grandfather's care.

The old King raised his grandson with care, even though he was a strange child, part mortal and part something else. Sometimes, when they sat in the garden, the *Táltos* King would see a dark cloud descend, almost to the ground, and he heard the boy talking to it.

"Who were you talking to, my darling?" he would ask later.

"My father sent a message. He misses me and wants me to be with him."

The King was sad to hear that, and yet, it happened every day the same. And then, one morning, the little Prince was gone.

"He disappeared in a cloud," the servants said.

The old King cried and cried. He could not contain his sorrow. He decided that he would confess it to the first person who asked what ailed him, and then he would end his own life. What he didn't know was that his daughter still loved him. Every day she demanded from her husband to be allowed to visit. She was close to getting permission, too, but one day a compassionate soldier asked the King what was wrong. The King, as soon as he unburdened his heart, fell to the ground dead.

The court was preparing for a funeral when the King's daughter finally returned in a great storm cloud and descended with her son under her arm. Everyone rejoiced to see the beautiful woman and her child. The Queen of the Clouds shook her cloak, and splashed some water on the King's face, waking the old *Táltos* immediately.

"My beloved child! You are home!"

People were startled, at first, to see the dead King come back to life. But as he embraced his daughter and grandson, they knew that this family had great power. They could do things mortals could not—even come back from the dead.

The Queen stayed with her father. They made a swing in the garden. The boy swung on it, and sometimes he and his grandfather sat on it together. One day they swung so high that the King's spurs caught a cloud and tore it open. A great flood poured down from the sky. It would have drowned everything, had the Queen not tossed her apron into it. The apron soaked up the flood, only leaving small lakes and ponds here and there. People loved her for it.

The boy grew up and became a great King. People still tell stories about the *Táltos* family today. I didn't know them, and I don't know where they live today, for this all happened long before I was born.

## Comments

Once again, we have a protagonist with a physical disability—one that does not stop her from becoming a queen, starting a family, and living happily ever after. Furicz János had a similar tale in his repertoire, in which a princess with no legs fell in love with the kind-hearted, garden-loving son of the enemy King. Their endearing "Romeo and Juliet" story reached a happy conclusion, and with the help of magic – unlike the *Táltos* Princess—she even got legs in the end.

Whether the Cloud King is the same person as the boy in the previous story or someone completely different is debatable, but he seems like a decent man regardless. I have often wondered about his first appearance. Anna says there was a "swooshing sound" (*zúgás*) from the sky, and then a basket descended to the palace. I am sure I'm not the only one who is reminded of a hot air balloon by this description. Sometimes, when I tell this story, I add the balloon, and how the court marveled at it. Other times, I hint at it with a cloud like I did in this text. The part where he takes the Princess to fly around is my own invention. I tell it to reflect the voyage from the previous tale, and to show that the Princess could learn to fly, even though she could not walk. While it is entirely possible that the ability of flight comes from the *táltos* powers, or the Cloud King's own purview, I enjoy elaborating on the idea of the early days of air travel.

*Táltos*, as I have mentioned before, is a term with shamanistic connotations. It generally means a person with innate supernatural powers. In the Hungarian tradition, children born with a tooth or with an extra finger are thought to become *táltos*. It is also a word used for magic horses (*táltosló*) as we have seen before. According to some traditions, the "táltos horse" was the drum used in shamanistic rituals that carried its owner on journeys into the spirit world. A "*táltos* king," however, is a unique concept; Furicz János had at least two stories that mentioned him as well.

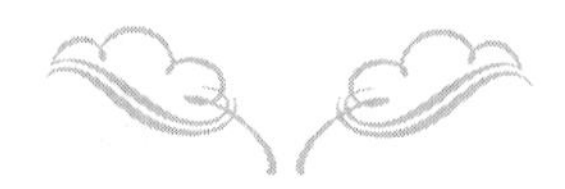

# The Boar and the Wheelbarrow

Once upon a time, across the magical Óperenciás Sea, there was a great forest. In the forest, there was a lake, and in the lake, grew a lot of water caltrops. By the lake stood the gamekeeper's house. It was his job to take care of the forest and its inhabitants.

One day, the King called for a big hunt in that forest since it was teeming with all kinds of animals. There were bears, boars, and other big game that wealthy lords enjoyed hunting. In the morning, the hunters gathered by the lake with all their greyhounds to make plans for the hunt. The King got a strange idea into his head. He insisted that he wanted to hunt alone. He wanted to spot and kill the game on his own with no help from servants or subjects. He told everyone to go in different directions and come back to the house in the evening to present what they killed.

No one really liked this idea. A king could not be left completely alone! Who would give him water? Who would carry his bag of food and ammunition? They can't just leave a king wandering about the forest! He could get lost or hurt or worse. With all of that in mind, the youngest hunter decided to step forward.

"Majesty, on my life, I will not leave you alone. I will go with you, and I promise to not shoot anything, not even a lame magpie, unless you say so. Just allow me to keep you company."

The King shooed him away, but the young man didn't leave; he kept following his King around. Finally, the King tossed his satchel at him.

"If you are not going to leave, then at least make yourself useful."

And that was that. The youngest hunter carried the satchel happily all day. They wandered among the trees, this way and that. They listened for animals. Suddenly, the hunter spotted a wild sow. He was just about to point it out to the King, when he noticed something very unusual. The sow was pushing a wheelbarrow! *That is strange*, thought the hunter, just as the King caught sight of it, too, and froze in surprise. They both gaped, noticing at the same time, that in the wheelbarrow, there was a beautiful little girl.

The King found his voice first.

"What a strange sow… Go and ask what it wants with that girl."

The sow was already steering the wheelbarrow their way and noticed how the King's face lit up when he saw the child. The King had no children of his own. He was already imagining how happy his wife would be if he took this little girl home.

"Majesty, I will leave this child in your care," said the sow, stepping away from the wheelbarrow. "She will bring much joy to you."

The sow left the child with the King, turned around and waded into the lake to eat some caltrops. The little girl laughed in the sunshine, clapping her hands. The King and the hunter watched her in awe. Her laughter was like music.

The King could not think about hunting anymore. He could barely wait to show the girl to everyone. Once he shook off the surprise, he sent the hunter after the sow to ask from where the child came, and who her parents were. The sow didn't even look up from chewing caltrops, she just said, "You'll find out if you live long enough," then refused to utter another word.

When the horn sounded the end of the hunt, everyone returned to the gamekeeper's house. When the King saw how many trophies the hunters had gathered, he felt a little ashamed, but no sooner did he look at the girl than his heart lightened again. He picked her up, and she snuggled against his shoulder. In the same moment, a bright light lit up the clearing around them, making the trees sparkle. The wheelbarrow was full of gemstones! The King and the hunters stared at it in awe, wondering just what kind of a child she was.

The youngest hunter was sent to the lake again to ask about the treasures. Who did they belong to?

"Oh, you, silly man. They belong to whoever raises that dear, little forest child," snorted the sow.

And that was that. The King got on his horse, the hunter handed the girl up to him, and then the hunter pushed the wheelbarrow all the way home. When they arrived at the castle, the King handed the girl to his wife's handmaid, so that she could be presented as a gift to the Queen.

The Queen was *not* happy. The moment she saw the child, she chased the handmaid out. Then the Queen went to her husband, throwing a tantrum, screaming that she wanted no one else's child, and he should take the child right back to wherever he'd found her. She would keep all her love and affections for her *own* children; she would not waste it on someone else's bastard. She was furious, but the King did not lose his patience.

He told the hunter, "Listen, Vencel, my wife doesn't know any better, but I can't help it. Please take this girl and raise her as if she were a princess. Take the wheelbarrow and the treasures and give her a happy life. But please, bring her to visit sometimes. I wish to see her grow. One day we will find out where she came from. I am sure."

So it happened that the Forest Foundling was raised in the hunter's home. She grew into a fair, young woman. The hunter built a castle for her and his family, and hired handmaidens to serve her as if she were a princess. Time flew by. The King loved the girl, and he was happy to see her grow. He didn't mind that she lived with the hunter. He visited them often. The Forest Foundling liked the King, too; she danced and sang whenever he was there. The arrangement was kept a secret, and only a precious few people knew about it.

In the meantime, the Queen also had a child, a son. When he grew up, he asked his father to take him along to visit the hunter. The Queen was hesitant to let him go as she did not want her son to mingle with all sorts of people. The King knew that the hunter's family could be trusted, and they would welcome the Prince with open arms. So he took his son along. The two young people, the Prince and the Forest Foundling, took one look at each other, and their faces lit up with joy. The King, the hunter, and the handmaids all watched them talk as if they had known each other all their lives. It was the most beautiful thing to behold. The hunter asked the Prince how they could possibly have so much to talk about.

"We were meant for each other, in this world and the next. Of course we get along well! The Forest Foundling knew I was going to come, and now she is happy that I am finally here. From this day on, I will visit every day, and, if my parents allow it, I will marry her. She is not a Forest Foundling; she is the daughter of the Sun King! She was cursed by the Cloud King because she was more beautiful than his own daughter. She is a princess. That is why she had all that treasure."

"I don't mind this at all," the old King chimed in when he heard his son speak. "But your mother will…"

"If she does, I will leave, and she will never see me again. The wind will bring news of my death when I die."

The King went to talk to his wife that night and told her what happened. The Queen threw a terrible tantrum, breaking everything she could. She screamed that there was no way her son, her beautiful only son, would marry the Forest Foundling. All the neighboring kings would have been happy to send their daughters to him since he was so handsome and was going to make such a fine king one day! But the King stood his ground this time. He kept telling her that if she did not relent, their son would leave and they would never see him again.

That scared the Queen since she did love her son. Next, she tried to bargain – couldn't they just let him keep visiting the girl, for a year or two, but not marry her? Youthful infatuation could burn out eventually.

But the King insisted that the two young ones loved each other dearly and truly. Eventually, for the love of her son, the Queen consented to the marriage. She did not even realize what joy she caused by doing so. When her son came in to thank her for her blessing, a dove flew into the room and heard them talk. It was none other than the wife of the Sun King, and she was happy to hear that the proud Queen had finally accepted her daughter as a daughter-in-law. In her joy, she shone so brightly that, as the Prince and his mother rode out to visit the hunter, they almost got a sunstroke—even with their parasols.

The girl greeted them at the door of the castle. She was so happy, she kissed the Queen's hands, and she kissed the train of her dress. The young couple matched perfectly. They were both from royal blood, and they were meant for each other. They had a splendid wedding, and they moved into the royal castle. The Forest Foundling had enough treasures of her own to match the King's.

After the wedding, the Princess asked her husband to take her to the lake where she had been found all those years ago. The Prince was happy to oblige. They took the old hunter, Vencel, with them since he knew the forest so well. When they got to the gamekeeper's house, the lake was gone. It had been there for more than 100 years, and now it was nowhere to be found. The gamekeeper told them that two or three weeks earlier the sun had shone so brightly that the lake dried up in a day.

"Where did the boars go?" inquired the hunter.

"They went to eat acorns in the forest. Only the oldest sow stayed, as she was too weak to go. She's right here behind the house."

Despite the gamekeeper claiming she was no great sight and almost dead already, they all went to see the old sow. The Princess even took a bowl of milk with her that she got from the gamekeeper's wife. As they went around the house, they found the old sow lying with her back to the sun, barely breathing. When the Princess saw her, she recognized the sow immediately. She hugged her, kissed her, and caressed her. The moment she did, the sow found her strength, jumped up, and snorted loudly enough that it made the trees shake. She was happy the Sun Princess didn't forget her. For that sow was no other than the Morning Star, and she had been a nurse to the little Princess, cursed by the Cloud King. As the old sow felt the love of the Princess, the coarse hide of thesow fell away, and she turned back into the Morning Star, winking at them happily as she rose to the sky.

Everyone rejoiced. Even the gamekeeper's wife did, and she was more than 1,000 weeks old! They all lived happily ever after. The Morning Star sometimes peeks in through their window, watching the Princess rock the cradle or the old Queen sing lullabies to her grandchildren.

**Comments**

This tale reminds me of Italo Calvino's *The Daughter of the Sun*. In that story, a Sun Princess is found in the woods by the King, raised away from the court, and she, too, marries the King's biological son in the end, although after a very different series of events. Furicz János had another tale about a Sun-daughter, and even one about Mistress Sunbeam, describing an entire royal family representing the Sun.

This tale, like many others in Anna's repertoire, focuses on the thoughts and emotions of its characters, rather than adventures involving magic. It becomes a veritable family drama in the end, before it resolves in a touching scene when the curse is fully broken. There is a very similar curse mentioned in another Hungarian folktale, *Gyöngyvirág Palkó* (Palkó Lily-of-the-Valley), where a jealous Tündér Ilona turns the daughter of the Dwarf King into a flower for being more beautiful than her, and then the flower is smuggled out of Fairyland by a loyal old nurse. The original text uses the term "boar" (*vaddisznó*) for the enchanted sow, referring to species rather than gender, and we only find out at the end of the story who she really is. I used 'sow' through the English translation to avoid confusion.

"Forest Foundling" is my translation for *Erdőnlelt*, "found in the forest." It is not a real name, merely one that hides the girl's identity until her royal-celestial parentage is revealed. The second time her curse is mentioned, Anna said *Szélkirály* (Wind King) instead of *Felhőkirály* (Cloud King), but, as we have seen in earlier stories, winds and clouds go hand in hand in this magical world.

And in case you were wondering… yes, you counted that right. The gamekeeper's wife was not yet 20 years old. I left that part in from the original text because I thought it was amusing.

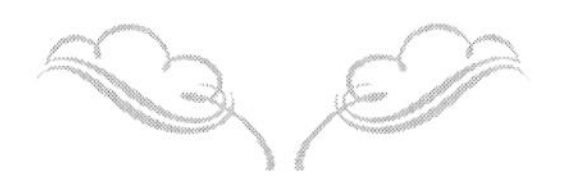

# Three Princesses and a Ring

Once upon a time, there was a king who had four great treasures: his three daughters and a ring. The three Princesses shared a loving, doting father, but they had been born from three different mothers. When the King first married, young and in love, he chose a fairy queen as a bride. They had a daughter and lived happily for a while. One day, however, the time of the fairies in our world came to an end, and the Queen, filled with sorrow, left with the rest of her people.

In time, the King married again. The new Queen was a wise woman, so wise that people started whispering about her being a witch. No matter how much the King loved her and their newborn daughter, the Queen knew that it was only a matter of time before the people would come for her. So, she went into exile and never returned.

The third time, the King played it safe. He married an ordinary mortal girl and had a third daughter with her.

The three Princesses were as different as their mothers, but the King loved them all equally. He loved them so much, in fact, that he had a ring made with three stones in it: blue sapphire for the clear eyes of the fairy Princess; black onyx for the sharp eyes of the wise Princess; and green emerald for the trusting eyes of the youngest Princess. The ring was his fourth and greatest treasure since it reminded him of all three of his beloved daughters.

One day, the King was strolling in his gardens, lost in thought. He wandered into a remote corner of the castle grounds, an overgrown and shadowy place with an ancient well that had been half-forgotten. The King leaned over the edge, wondering how deep the well was, and, as he absent-mindedly twirled the ring around his finger, the ring suddenly slipped off and fell into the abyss.

The King was devastated. He wanted his treasure back. He ordered his servants to search the well, but even though they descended into it with ropes and torches, no one could find or even see the bottom. Whatever they threw into it, it never made a sound. The King raged and cried and promised gifts and titles to whoever could retrieve the ring from the well. Princes, knights, and heroes came from all corners of the kingdom. Some of them spent days down in the well. Some of them never returned. But even the ones who did, did so empty-handed. The ring was lost.

One day, a stranger, who was tall, dark and handsome, appeared in the garden and offered to help the King.

"Your Highness, I promise to return your ring, if you promise to give me your eldest daughter as a wife."

The King nodded without hesitation and waved the stranger towards the well, but the stranger didn't move.

"First, I would like to get a kiss from my bride," he said, "up front – for courage. It is likely I will never return."

The King sighed and called for his eldest daughter. The Princess appeared in the door of the castle, took one look at the stranger, and screamed.

"Father, what is *that* man doing in our garden?!"

"He promised to return my ring, daughter. Come, give him a kiss before he goes down the well."

"I will *not!*" the Princess stomped her foot. "That man is the King of the Devils!"

Her father's eyes grew wide.

"How do you know?"

"Father, did you forget that my mother was a fairy? I can see what he truly is. And I would rather die than marry him!"

With that, the eldest Princess turned and ran back inside the castle.

"Silly girl," the stranger smiled. "Well, Your Majesty, if the eldest won't have me, I'll take the second Princess."

The King called for his second daughter to give the stranger a kiss, but the moment she appeared in the doorway, she screamed as well.

"Papa! That man is the Devil!"

"How do you know?"

"He smells like sulfur!"

The second Princess still remembered her mother and her vast knowledge of herbs and potions. She recognized the smell of Hellfire and ran back inside the castle.

The King sighed, annoyed with his daughters, and called for the youngest one. The youngest Princess, you remember, was the daughter of a mere mortal. She was not as sharp as her sisters, and she was even a little bit short-sighted. But as she walked out of the castle and saw the stranger, she screamed just as loud.

"Papa! That man is the Devil!"

"How can you possibly know?!" demanded the King angrily.

"Papa, *he has hooves!!*"

Devil or no devil, the King was at his wits' end.

"I don't care who he is! He won't return my ring until he gets a kiss."

"Well then, father, you can kiss him yourself!"

The Princess marched back into the castle, leaving her father and the stranger alone.

"I will take a kiss for the ring," the stranger said, "even if it is from Your Majesty. And when I return the treasure, I expect to marry the youngest Princess."

The King was so set on getting his ring back that he agreed, and – with some hesitation – he planted a kiss on the Devil's lips. In that instant, the visitor disappeared down the well, and returned not a moment later, holding the King's ring. The King was happier than ever! But no matter how he tried to put it back on his finger, the ring wouldn't fit.

"Your hands are swollen from nerves," the stranger suggested. "Your youngest daughter can smooth your fingers, and the ring will fit again."

The King sent for his daughter instantly; but the messenger returned saying that the youngest Princess was getting dressed, and if the King wanted a word, he would have to go to her. Mumbling to himself, very displeased, the King climbed the stairs to the tower where the Princesses lived. Opening the door, he saw a coffin in the middle of the room, and the youngest Princess lying in it, dressed for her own funeral.

"Papa, if you make me marry the Devil, I will die! And he didn't even give you the real ring!"

"He didn't?"

The other Princesses walked up to their father and pointed at the ring.

"Look closer, Papa. It can't be the real one! All three stones are there, but they are in the wrong order. Look!"

The King looked, and realized that they were right. He suddenly felt ashamed of himself. When he had the ring made, it had been to remind him of what he treasured the most, his three daughters—the very daughters that he was willing to give away for a piece of jewelry. He opened the window and threw it out.

The ring fell, and as it fell, it turned into a large frog. It just so happened that one of the King's stable boys was hunting in the garden for frogs. He caught the fat one that landed at his feet and took it to the kitchens. As it was cut open, the real ring rolled out of its belly!

The stable boy ran to the King and the Princesses immediately.

"Your Majesty! I found your ring!"

The King saw that *this* ring was the real one and embraced the stable boy with gratitude. The Princesses also rejoiced; especially the youngest one, who just happened to look at the boy a little too long, and the boy looked back at her. Even the King noticed.

"Do you wish to marry one of my daughters, my son? I did promise a reward to whoever returned my ring,"

"I couldn't hope for such a thing, Your Majesty. I am just a servant.

I don't have the means to care for a princess and give her everything she deserves."

"Oh, but I also promised part of my kingdom," the King hurried to add with a smile. After that, no one needed convincing at all. The stable boy became a prince and a married man, all on the same day.

On the day of the wedding, however, an unexpected visitor appeared. The Devil had been waiting by the well for his bride ever since the King left him there. When he heard music coming from the castle, he thought that they were preparing for his own wedding with the Princess. When the Devil appeared and saw that she was marrying someone else, he grew angry. He tried to grab the Princess and drag her away. There was a commotion, people started screaming. The only person who acted fast enough was the groom. He drew a sword, beat the Devil away, dragged him back to the garden, and threw him down the well. His first order as the Prince was for the well to be boarded up, walled in, and buried under rocks, so the Devil would never return.

Some say the bottomless well is still there somewhere in an overgrown corner of some castle's garden, buried and forgotten. We don't know for sure. What we do know, however, is this: the three clever Princesses, the Prince, and the old King all lived happily ever after.

### Comments

This story was included in the first published collection of Anna's tales, under the title "The Bottomless Well." It looks somewhat different in the original. I have been telling it for years, and the version above is how I tell it now. In the original text, Anna begins with the description of the bottomless well and the King losing his ring; we only find out about the background of the royal family later. The order of the Princesses is also different. Originally, the youngest is fairy-born, and the eldest is human, with a "wise woman" or "enchantress" in-between. I added the background story about the three queens as it made the most sense to me. The fairies leaving the world is a common motif in Hungarian tradition, as I have mentioned before, and so is, sadly, witch-hunting. In the original story, the youngest Princess sees the Devil's true nature; the middle Princess notices the hooves, and the oldest one smells the sulfur (since she is human and short-sighted). I switched these around because in live telling the most obvious clue—HOOVES!—works like a charm as a punch line. The story does say that the King had three stones on the ring for the eyes of the Princesses (I loved that the first time I read it), but I added the colors myself. One element I discarded is that the original text calls the Devil "Gypsy-looking." That did not sit well with me, therefore, I changed to the formulaic "tall, dark, and handsome."

In terms of story motifs, this tale is one of the most unique from Pályuk Anna. It includes a lot of known elements – promising a girl to the Devil, a mysterious well, three princesses, and kisses demanded – but it does not fit any established folktale type. The closest point of comparison I could find was a legend about the well in the castle of Munkács (Mukacheve), where the Devil is tricked into digging a well. When his payment is refused, he disappears in the well forever. The story also somewhat alludes to *The Frog-King* known from the Grimm's collection, but more so in imagery than in actual plot (the "Frog King" folktale type, AaTh 440, exists in the Hungarian tradition in several versions). It sounds like a play on the type of tales where princesses are handed out as prizes willy-nilly, and it is smart about it, too.

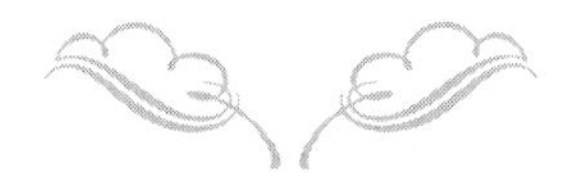

# The Daughter of the Iron-Nosed Witch

Once upon a time, far away where the sky touches the earth, there was an old, iron-nosed witch. She was so hideous that people were afraid to go near her house, even during the day. Sometimes they could not avoid it because her house, unfortunately, was right by the road. She also had a beautiful daughter, so beautiful that when she sat outside to comb her golden hair, even the moon paused in the sky to admire her. The daughter did not have a mirror, so she used to lean over a small pond to see her own reflection. Whoever saw her went hot and cold with love.

The witch guarded her daughter jealously. She locked her inside the house with six locks whenever she had to leave. She traveled a lot, given her profession. But even like this, she could not keep the girl away from prying eyes.

One day a Prince passed by, hunting, and heard singing from inside the house. He sent his huntsman to see who was singing, mortal or angel, for it was such a beautiful voice. The huntsman looked in through the window, saw the girl, and stayed there as if he had been glued to the wall. The Prince sent another huntsman, and the same thing happened to him, too; now there were two of them staring in the window, unable to move. The Prince got bored waiting. He was just about to follow them when the witch caught up to him.

"Are you also looking for the source of the singing, grandmother?" the Prince asked cheerfully.

"Good of you to greet me like that, for if you didn't, you would be stuck to the wall like those two idiots you sent earlier. But you shall not see who sings anyway, for she is my daughter," the witch snarled at him showing her yellow teeth. And then she ran away from the stunned Prince.

*How can such a hideous hag have a daughter with such a beautiful voice?* The Prince wondered. But he soon had other things to think about for he realized that he could not move… at all! The witch had bound his sinews with a spell; he could not take a step forward or backward. He stood there all night, praying that someone would find him.

At midnight, the girl went out to the pond to brush her hair. She could only sneak outside at night, while her mother was asleep. The moment she stepped outside, she noticed the two huntsmen and took pity on them. She brushed them with a broom, and they immediately peeled off the wall and took off running to find the Prince. They were stunned to see him close by, standing like a statue, but staring towards the pond none the less. Following his gaze, the two hunters almost went blind from beauty. So, there they stood, all three of them, watching as the girl brushed her hair and went back into the house.

The huntsmen tried to move the Prince, but they couldn't. He was rooted to the spot. So, they agreed that one of them would go home and bring horses to drag him away, and soldiers to raze the witch's house to the ground. By the morning, the huntsman returned with four horses and two strong men. First, they tied the Prince to two horses, but he didn't even budge. Second, they tied him to four. The Prince roared in pain. It was likely that his legs would break off sooner than the ground would let him go. The roaring brought the witch outside, and she began to cackle happily. The cackle lured the girl outside as well. She felt pity for the Prince.

"How can you do this, mother? Do you wish to kill him like all the others?"

The witch waved a hand and went back into the house, happily chuckling. The moment the strong men saw that the girl was outside and the witch was in, they grabbed up the entire house and tossed it into the pond. The pond was bottomless, and the house with the iron-nosed witch sank away from sight like a stone.

The curse on the Prince was broken the moment the girl touched him. He was free, and so was she, as there were no more locks on the door. The Prince asked her to marry him immediately, and she agreed with a happy heart. They had a great wedding; everyone drank, ate, and danced as much as they could. They lived happily ever after, the Queen singing and the King laughing. They were happy, and their happiness warmed everyone around them. That is what good kings do.

### Comments

This story reminds me of the "girl in the tower" type folktales (ATU 310), most generally known as Grimm's *Rapunzel.* While the most commonly recognized visual, the long braid in the tower, is missing from this version, we still get multiple mentions of the girl's golden locks, and her captivity in the witch's house. This folktale type, while very popular in Western Europe and the Mediterranean, is virtually unknown in the Hungarian tradition.

The iron-nosed witch (*vasorrú bába*) is one of those characters in Hungarian folktales that every child recognizes. She is our most popular villain, an old hag with great magical powers and a somewhat baffling facial feature that has a very cool backstory. While most witches (*boszorkány*) are mortal women with powers, the *bába* (much like the *böjti boszorkány* in the first tale of this book) is usually a completely different, supernatural being. In related beliefs from Turkic and Finno-Ugric peoples, "iron-nosed" or "iron-tooth" referred to spirit beings whose wooden idols were often smeared with food and other offerings on special occasions. To keep the wood from rotting, they covered their facial area with metal ornaments. Sometimes the iron-nosed witch is the Mother of Dragons or some other relation of villainous characters. In Rusyn folktales, she takes on a similar role to Grimm's *Mother Holle*. In Hungarian youth slang, she is most often referenced as, "I faceplanted like an iron-nosed witch on a magnetic table." Folklore is alive and well.

# Sources and Further Reading

**Archival Materials:**
Kocsisné Szirmai Fóris Mária's collection of Pályuk Anna's tales can be found in the Archives of the Hungarian Museum of Ethnography, under EA 4203, 9562, and 12665.


**Hungarian folktale collections featuring tales from Pályuk Anna:**

Kovács, Ágnes – Kocsisné Szirmai Fóris, Mária. *Felsőtiszai népmesék.* Debrecen: Alföldi Magvető, 1956.

Mészöly, Miklós. *A tengelépő cipő.* Budapest: Móra Ferenc Ifjúsági Könyvkiadó, 1959.

Kocsisné Szirmai Fóris, Mária. *Csodacsupor.* Budapest: Móra Ferenc Ifjúsági Könyvkiadó, 1968.

Simonits, Mária – Cs. Meggyes, Mária. *Szélanyó keresztlánya.* Budapest: Móra Ferenc Ifjúsági Könyvkiadó, 1986.

Varga, Domokos. *Ritkaszép magyar népmesék.* Budapest: Hét Krajcár Kiadó, 1998.


Tales That Appear in Print Here for the First Time:
*The Stolen Apples, The Maiden With the Red-gold Hair, The Sleepy Lady, The Poor Man and the Three Ladies, The Joy of the Princess, The Woodcutter's Luck, Who Owns the Golden Apples? What did the Little Pig do in the Winter? Mistress Tuberose, Touch-me-not, The King of the Birchwood, Little Orphan, Szelemen in the Apple Orchard, The Daughter of the Iron-nosed Witch.*


**English-Language Folktale Collections Mentioned in Comments:**

Basile, Giambattista – Zipes, Jack. *Giambattista Basile's Tale of Tales, or Entertainment for Little Ones.* Detroit: Wayne State University Press, 2014.

Calvino, Italo. *Italian Folktales.* New York: Harcourt Brace Jovanovich, 1980.

Campbell, J. F. *Popular Tales of the West Highlands*. London: Alexander Gardner, 1890.

Colarusso, John – Mayor, Adrienne. *Nart sagas: Ancient myths and legends of the Circassians and Abkhazians*. Princeton: Princeton University Press, 2016.

Cooper, David L. *Traditional Slovak folktales*. London: M. E. Sharpe, 2001.

Fillmore, Parker. *Czechoslovak Fairy Tales*. Rahway: The Quinn & Boden Company, 1919.

Heiner, Heidi Anne. *Rapunzel and other maiden in the tower tales from around the world*. SurLaLune Press, 2009.

Thompson, Stith. *Motif-index of folk-literature*. Bloomington: Indiana University Press, 1955-58.

Uther, Hans-Jörg. *The types of international folktales*. Helsinki: Academia Scientiarum Fennica, 2004.

Zipes, Jack. *The original folk & fairy tales of the Brothers Grimm: The complete first edition*. Princeton: Princeton University Press, 2014.

**Hungarian and Ukrainian Folktales Published in English:**

Benedek, Elek. *The tree that reached the sky*. Budapest: Corvina, 1999.

Bilenko, Anton – Adamovich, Roman. *Ukrainian folk tales*. Kiev: Dnipro Publishers, 1974.

Biro, Val. *Hungarian folk-tales*. Oxford: Oxford University Press, 1992.

Bloch, Marie Halun et al. *Ukrainian folktales*. New York: Hippocrene Books, 1999.

Dégh, Linda. *Folktales of Hungary*. Chicago: The University of Chicago Press, 1965.

Dégh, Linda. *Hungarian folktales: the art of Zsuzsanna Palkó*. University Press of Mississippi, 1996.

Hoffmann, Margaret - Bíró, Gyuri. *The money hat and other Hungarian folk tales*. Philadelphia: The Westminster Press, 1969.

Illyés, Gyula. *Once upon a time: forty Hungarian folk-tales*. Budapest: Corvina Press, 1964.

Jones, W. Henry. *The folk-tales of the Magyars*. London: E. Stock, 1889.

Manning-Sanders, Ruth. *The glass man and the golden bird: Hungarian folk and fairy tales*. Oxford: Oxford University Press, 1968.
Molnár, Irma. *One-time dog market at Buda – and other Hungarian folk-tales*. North Haven, CT: Linnet Books, 2001.
Oparenko, Christina. *Ukrainian folk-tales*. Oxford: Oxford University Press, 1996.
Orczy, Emma. *Old Hungarian fairy-tales*. London: Dean & Son / Wolf & Co, 1895.
Ortutay, Gyula. *Hungarian folk tales*. Budapest: Corvina, 1962.
Suwyn, Barbara – Kononenko, Natalie. *The magic egg and other tales from the Ukraine*. Englewood, CO: Libraries Unlimited, 1997.
*The flying ship and other Ukrainian folk tales*. Toronto: Holt, Rinehart, and Winston of Canada, 1975.
*The princess that saw everything* (Mindent látó királylány). Budapest: Móra kiadó, 1998.
Wass, Albert. *Selected Hungarian folk tales*. Astor Park, FL: Danubian Press, Inc, 1972.